Violet Dawn

Alex Hyland

Published by Accent Press Ltd 2019
Octavo House
West Bute Street
Cardiff
CF10 5LJ

www.accentpress.co.uk

ISBN 9781786153784
eISBN 9781786153777

Printed and bound in Great Britain by Clays Ltd,
Elcograf S.p.A

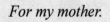

For my mother.

1

The tiny receiver in my left ear buzzed with static as I weaved through the guests.

Agent Willard's voice crackled into my head. 'Do you see him?'

I searched the crowds, but there had to be five hundred people in the house. A fancy party on North Lake Shore, the place was packed wall-to-wall with Chicago's finest.

'Answer me,' said Willard.

'Not yet,' I replied. The mic in my tie relayed the message.

I headed into the main reception and a thick soup of conversations and laughter. I glanced around the room – the aftermath of some fashion show. A raised catwalk stretched across the floor, willowy models drifting through the crowds. It might have been the kind of party that I'd liked to have hung out at for a while, but not tonight. I needed to get out as quickly as I could.

I slowed as I caught sight of the party's host – a wiry little Chanel spider named Marianne Shelby. I didn't know that much about her – in her eighties, one of Chicago's rich widows. She stood arm-in-arm with some beady-eyed boyfriend who looked even older than she did. Jesus, they brought new meaning to the term 'carbon dating'.

'Where are we?' said Willard. 'Do you see him yet?'

I kept my eyes on the guests milling around Shelby, but the guy we were looking for, Chris Joseph, was nowhere. I checked my watch. Shit, we were running out of time.

'Alright, I'm going to get myself thrown out,' I said.

'Are you sure?' Willard replied.

'We can't wait.'

'Be careful.'

This needed to be done gently. I couldn't start a fight or anything else that might risk me getting detained by the police. I grabbed a glass of champagne from one of the busboys, then weaved toward Shelby. She and her boyfriend were introducing a small circle of guests to some artsy-looking brunette in her twenties – the fashion designer, I guessed.

A guy in his fifties kissed Shelby on the cheek. 'It was a stunning show, Marianne. Congratulations.'

'Thank you,' she replied. 'But it was Jemma's night.'

The guy nodded at the artsy girl. 'Your designs are spectacular.'

As Jemma smiled gratefully, I barged my way into the circle.

'Hey, everybody, I'm Rick!' I said.

All eyes on me – all of them antagonistic, except for Shelby, who smiled.

2

'Good evening, Rick,' she said.

'Yeah,' I replied. 'A good evening it certainly is. Nice house. Great party, by the way.'

'Thank you. Did you enjoy the show?'

'Oh, it was great.' I took a deep gulp of champagne then glanced at Jemma. 'Although... you need to get some regular-looking girls up on that catwalk. Just for your own sanity, you know.'

Jemma stared at me. 'My own sanity?'

'Yeah, you got these gorgeous models, but so what? They already look great. It's like getting Jesus to sell surfboards, he can walk on the fucking water anyhow.'

A moment of silence. Good.

Shelby eyed me coolly. 'Sorry, you are?'

'Rick. Sullivan.'

'Yes, and you're a friend of?'

'Oh, no one really. I'm a blogger. Celebrity gossip, you know, who's had their tits done. I heard about your party thing here, thought I'd see what was going on.'

'I see. Do you mind me asking how you got in?'

I laughed. 'Yeah, I know, I slipped past your security guys. Don't worry, I'm not an asshole.'

Shelby's boyfriend smiled politely to the others. 'Excuse me.'

I watched as he headed off into the crowd, then I stepped away from the circle myself. 'Anyhow, I'm going to get another drink,' I said. 'Anybody want anything? Hmmm? No? OK.'

I headed toward the main hallway, readying myself for my imminent departure. I made sure I stayed in Shelby's line of sight, then glanced at the main door. I

3

needed to get him outside where it was quiet.

'You need to get moving,' said Willard.

'I know.'

'The plane's already landed.'

'I'm on it!'

A huge security guy appeared beside Shelby. Six-two, mixed race – this was the guy, this was Chris Joseph. Shelby spoke to him for a moment, then pointed in my direction.

He started making his way toward me.

'OK, I got him, he's coming,' I said.

'Fast!' said Willard.

I eyed Joseph's suit. Prada. Silk weave, slim fit, I knew it well. Three pockets, one internal in the left panel.

Joseph stopped in front of me. 'Rick Sullivan?'

I grinned at him. 'Yeah.'

'If you could follow me, please.'

'Why, where are we going?'

He ushered me toward the main door. 'You're not on the guest list.'

'I'm press.'

'This is a private party.'

I ground to a stubborn halt as he opened the main door. He grabbed me by the arm.

'Hey, get your hands off me!' I said.

He gripped me harder as he opened the main door.

'Hey, you're hurting me man, Jesus!'

As he pushed me out into the front courtyard, my hand slid inside his jacket. Leather slim-fold wallet – I had it in a second – but I wasn't done yet. I purposely slipped and fell to the ground.

'Motherfucker!' I said. I eyed him intently. 'What's your name?'

'Just get going.'

I got to me feet. 'No, no, what's your name? You nearly broke my goddamn arm! I'm going to fucking sue your ass!'

He laughed. 'You're not going to do anything.'

'Your name! Come on! I'll get it anyhow. I'll subpoena that boss of yours if I have to, the bitch!'

And that was it – no matter how pathetic I might have looked to him, he wouldn't risk any hassle for Shelby.

'You know who Marianne Shelby is?' he said. 'I'd let it go if I were you.'

'I mean it!' I said.

He laughed to himself. 'Chris Joseph. Good luck with it, fucker.'

The moment he turned and headed back into the house, I ran for my car.

'You get it?' I said.

'Yeah,' replied Willard. 'I'm sending it to your phone now.'

'How much time have we got?'

'Twenty minutes. He's heading north on 94.'

Shit, I needed to get to Glencoe fast. I started up the car, screeched past the park, then swung into the first road that took me north.

'OK I'm heading north on Pine,' I said.

'Pine?' said Willard. 'Hang on, Pine's one-way!'

'I'm only going one way!'

5

I hit the accelerator and weaved through the oncoming traffic. As car horns blared all around me, I grabbed Joseph's wallet and shook out its contents. Cash and cards spilled across the passenger seat. Among the cards was one that looked like a blank strip of aluminum. I picked it up – there was a tiny serial number etched into its surface. Headlights blinded me for a second – I swerved the car into the next lane.

'I've got it,' I said.

'Are you sure?' replied Willard.

'Yeah.'

I made sure there were no police units on my tail, then floored the pedal – the oncoming headlights accelerating into a fluid blur. I weaved through the traffic, then swung the car out onto the empty air of the highway, tires screeching as I sped north toward Glencoe and the rows of limestone mansions that sat on Lake Michigan.

I tried to calm my breathing, but there were just minutes left to us now. We'd only found out an hour ago that Chris Joseph worked security for one other client aside from Marianne Shelby – a shipping contractor named David Massa. The agency had been monitoring Massa for a couple of months. I don't know what shit he was involved in, but my orders were simple – get into Massa's house and photograph the most recent entries in a green suede diary on his desk. Although his house wasn't that far from Shelby's, he was arriving back in Chicago tonight and the guy had landed early – which meant I was in the usual shit the agency liked to drop me in.

I followed the shore until the city lights faded, then weaved into the quiet suburb. Nothing but trees and tastefully lit driveways, the houses here well hidden from the roads. I turned down a leafy side street, then came to a stop beside the twelve-foot brick wall that surrounded Massa's house. His chateau-style villa looked dark and still, a sprawling shadow rising above the cypress trees beyond the wall.

'I'm outside the house,' I said.

'He's coming off the 94,' said Willard. 'You've got eight minutes tops.'

The wall around the house had two gates – a main and a service entrance, each granting access via a security panel in the wall. As I ran over to the service entrance, I checked my phone – the message from Willard was waiting. I took a quick look around me, then brushed Joseph's security card against the panel by the gate. An LED screen in the panel flickered into life.

A request written on the screen: *Please say your name.*

I held my phone up to the screen and played the message that Willard had sent me.

'Chris Joseph,' came the voice from my phone.

The screen went blank for a moment, just a tiny blue dot circling in its center, indicating that the voice recognition system was processing.

The gate slid silently open. No complications. Good.

'I'm in,' I said.

'His office is to the rear, overlooking the lake,' said

Willard.

I darted through the gardens toward a door at the side of the house. A similar access panel in the wall by the door. I swiped Joseph's card, then played his voice into the panel. The security system processed the voice.

The door clicked open. I slipped inside.

Next to no light in the house, just a thick weave of shadows – windows and chairs silhouetted against the night glow of the lake. I crept through the darkness, following the windows around the rear of the house. I passed through a video screening room, a huge, lifeless TV on the wall beside me. Beyond the TV, an open door led into a large circular office overlooking the water. I could see a laptop and phone sitting on a wooden desk by the windows. I ran over to the desk and opened its single drawer. Sitting among a pile of documents at the bottom was the green suede diary.

'I got it,' I said.

'OK,' said Willard. 'We're looking for anything that looks like arrival dates, flight details.'

I opened the diary. The pages were crammed with complex entries, shorthand and abbreviations. The guy evidently didn't trust computers.

'There's a lot of stuff in here,' I said.

'Just photograph the pages back until the twelfth, then put it back where you found it.'

I took out my phone, turned on the flash, and started photographing the pages. As I did, my mood calmed a little. Massa would be back any minute, but things were running smoothly – the door, the diary, it was all just as the agency had said. I may not have liked the guys at Southwest Intelligence much, but they knew what they were doing.

I finished photographing the diary, then carefully placed it back in the desk. I closed the drawer, then looked around for the master security panel. I needed to delete Chris Joseph's arrival this evening. As I scanned the office walls, I heard a door close somewhere in the house.

I froze as I gazed into the darkness. 'Where's Massa?' I whispered.

'Four minutes away.'

I listened carefully. Footsteps – coming from beyond the video screening room. Whoever it was, they were heading this way. I ducked back into the shadows of the office.

'Someone's here,' I whispered.

'Are you sure?' said Willard.

I kept my eyes on the screening room – blue light erupting from the TV. I stayed absolutely still as a guy in a white bathrobe drifted over to the sofa and sat down. Mid-thirties. Latino-looking. He ran a hand through his soaking wet hair, then placed a glass of whiskey on the corner table. He grabbed the TV remote and started browsing the news channels.

I kept my voice low. 'OK, I've got a Latino male. Mid-thirties. Five-ten.'

'Has he seen you?'

'No.' I glanced at another door in the office by the windows. 'I think I can get out without him knowing.'

'Wait,' said Willard. 'Latino?'

'Yeah.'

'Wait,' said Willard. He went quiet for a moment as he rustled through papers on his desk.

'He's watching TV,' I said. 'I can get out.'

'Five-ten?' said Willard. 'Can you confirm a burn mark on his right arm?'

I tried to see more clearly through the screening room door, but the guy was slouched back on the sofa.

'I can't see,' I said.

Willard's voice became muffled as he spoke to someone else on a phone.

I glanced at the windows overlooking the lake. 'Willard…' I said.

'Wait,' he replied.

As he continued his other conversation, I kept my eyes on the screening room.

'You see the burn mark yet?' he said to me.

'No.'

He spoke again into the phone. 'No confirmation,' he said. He paused a moment. 'Understood.' He put down the phone.

Willard's voice low and clear in my earpiece. 'Kill him, Michael.'

It felt like a hammer blow. 'What?'

'I say again, kill him. This is the target. The information in the diary was his arrival plans in the US… the plans obviously changed. We won't find him again. We need to do this now.'

'Willard…'

'That's an order, Michael.'

I just stared at the guy.

Fuck.

My job at the agency was to just lift keys and wallets, gain information. But this was the second time I'd ended up in the direct vicinity of one of their targets, and the agency seemed to have no problem asking me to handle it. I'd been saved from pulling the trigger the first time by the arrival of the target's family, but I doubted I'd be that lucky tonight. I'd killed before, admittedly – the guys responsible for my brother's death – but this was different. There was no anger or desire in this, nothing human about it I could retreat into. It was too cold. Alien. In the movies, James Bond kills a guy then strolls off and orders himself a Martini. The reality for me was I'd probably spend the next two weeks shivering under a duvet, clutching at an industrial-sized bucket of vodka.

Willard's voice in my ear. 'Michael!'

I kept my eyes on the guy.

'I can't confirm it's him,' I said.

'The burn mark, it's on his inner right arm. It should look like an arrow.'

I couldn't see it – not that it would have made any difference even if I could. I was looking for a way out of this, and Willard knew it.

'You need to do this now,' he said.

'Who is he?' I said. 'What he's done.'

'That's not your business.'

'Killing isn't my business either.'

'You need to do it now!' He paused a moment, tempering the frustration in his voice. 'We can't afford this guy leaving the house, trust me.'

11

I closed my eyes. Fuck.

I took a deep breath. For God and country. Tomorrow was the prize.

'Michael!'

'OK,' I said. 'OK.'

I reached for the pistol in my jacket, gazed at it, then slowly raised the barrel. I tried to calm myself – quiet, deep breaths as I crept toward the screening room. The guy was steeped in the blaze of the TV screen. As he browsed another news channel, I reached the screening room door and aimed the gun at him.

'Don't move,' I said.

He spun round, caught sight of the pistol in my hand, then froze.

'Show me your right arm,' I said.

He stayed quiet. Kept his eyes on me.

'Your right arm! Show me!'

The room fell black as the TV went dead... a shadow leaping through the darkness toward me. I pulled the trigger, then collapsed as the guy crashed into me – his body crushing me to the floor, my pistol slipping across the boards. The blood hammered through my veins as I grabbed hold of him. I wrapped an arm around his neck, clenched a fist, then went still. The guy wasn't moving. His head remained drooped against my shoulder.

My eyes adjusted to the darkness, and I could see it – the bullet had caught him in the left side of his face. An ugly exit wound had torn out the back of his head. I rolled his body off me, my gaze fixed on the fading hint of life in his eyes.

The blood pouring down his face as his expression turned hollow.

Willard's voice in my ear. 'Michael!'

I couldn't breathe.

'Michael, what's happened?'

I slowly reached across his body and rolled up the right sleeve of his robe.

Nothing.

My hands shook as I checked his other arm. Fuck.

'No burn mark,' I said. 'There's no burn mark, Willard!'

'Are you sure?'

'Jesus…'

'Get out. Just get out!'

The whisper of a car pulling up at the front of the house. I gazed back at the guy – the blood pooling across the boards beneath his head. His eyes empty.

I scrambled to my feet, grabbed the pistol from the floor, then tore through the rooms. Out into the gardens. My head burning as I tumbled toward the cold, numbing darkness of the lake.

13

2

I raised the vodka bottle to my lips as I sat on the floor of Arlen Connell's kitchen. I took a deep mouthful, then closed my eyes and rested my head against the cupboards. The air conditioning blowing rivulets around my fingers. The lawn sprinklers spitting into life outside in the manicured New Hampshire garden. I didn't feel the pain any more. Nineteen hours since Massa's house, and I was numb. Just a faulty appliance sitting in Arlen's kitchen.

I'd come straight from Chicago to see him. Arlen ran Southwest Intelligence and was the only guy I could talk to, certainly the only one who'd listen. Willard and the others were little more than ghosts – faceless figures detached from anything resembling humanity. Then again, when you're in the very quiet business of government-sanctioned killing, I guess it pays to be that way. There was no room here for prayers and sympathy.

Joining them wasn't a choice that I'd made lightly. I'd known pretty much from the outset what Southwest's remit was, however, Arlen had sold it to me in the name of national security, and the assurance that I'd have nothing do with the wet end of the business. My job would be to gain information; to serve as part of the nebulous infrastructure that supported the agency's hitmen. But the job was changing now. I'd been with them for nearly a year, and they were pushing me into new territory. It was a mess. I wasn't a hitman. I didn't have the heart for it. The problem was, I had the talent. Being a hitman had nothing to do with how well you could aim a rifle. When was the last time you heard of someone being taken out by a rooftop assassin? JFK, maybe. Assassinations were performed up close. Hidden away from public scrutiny as robberies or domestic incidents. Being an assassin was all about gaining access, and, unfortunately, that's what I could offer. It may have been in the name of national security, but I couldn't stand another day of it.

I heard the house's elevator stir into life. I stayed slumped in the shadows and kept my eyes on the hallway. The rattle of the elevator doors opening. The gentle hum of an electric motor as Arlen steered his wheelchair into the kitchen. I stayed low and just watched him.

It had been eight months since I'd seen him face-to-face. He'd been ill in that time – heart problems, I think, but I wasn't sure. Either way, he was confined to a wheelchair now. Not that I had an ounce of sympathy for him. He looked healthy enough to me. A well-fed flush in his cheeks – his bushy gray mustache neatly trimmed. As he headed toward the fridge, he kept his bespectacled attention fixed on an LED screen attached to one of the chair's armrests. I couldn't see the screen, but I could hear a guy's voice coming from it – another one of his agents by the sound of it. Arlen spoke briefly with him about some job in Phoenix, then signed off the conversation.

He grabbed a sandwich from the fridge, then wheeled himself over to the cutlery drawer. As his wheelchair scraped and clanked against the cupboard doors, I closed my eyes and took another mouthful of vodka. It felt like we were the low-rent X-Men, and useless with it.

'It was the wrong guy,' I said.

My voice shook him. I was glad that it did.

He eyed me for a moment, his shock at my presence quickly turning to anger.

'Michael,' he said. 'How did…'

He stopped himself. He was going to hire me because I was a good pickpocket, then ask how I got into his house?

'It was the wrong fucking guy,' I said.

He sighed heavily, then nodded.

'Who was he?' I asked.

'We don't know yet. But chances are he was an associate of the target.'

'Chances are?'

'You didn't kill an innocent man.'

'You know that?'

He glanced at the kitchen door. His wife was upstairs – I hadn't seen her that evening, but I'd heard her.

He took a deep breath, then glanced back at me.

'I can see you've had a drink,' he said.

'Don't worry, I'm not staying.'

16

I kept my eyes on him as I got to my feet.

'I'm out, Arlen. I can't do this any more.'

He nodded thoughtfully to himself.

'It's a shame,' he said. 'You're a good agent.'

'I'm not a killer.'

'I would probably have to disagree with you on that.'

'I'm not going to let you turn me into one either.'

He laughed to himself. 'Turn you into one? You killed the Bragers long before you met me, Michael.'

'That was for my brother!'

'Call it what you like, you had blood on your hands and bodies behind you.'

'That makes me a killer? You've got wheels and a talking display, that don't make you a fucking BMW!'

His wife called out from upstairs. 'Arlen?'

'It's fine!' he called back. 'It's fine, Lucy, it's work. Go back to bed.'

We waited a moment for the door upstairs to close.

I rubbed some life into my face. 'You know, when I signed up for this, I thought I'd be doing some good.'

'You are,' he said. 'But it's complicated. And it's hard and painful. And it should be. Death isn't something we should ever manage lightly.'

He wheeled himself closer to me. 'You're upset. I understand. But why exactly? If I can show you that the man you killed yesterday was as guilty as the target, will that set the situation straight? They're bomb-makers, Michael. Massa doesn't know who he's getting involved with.'

But I didn't give a shit. Even if the guy deserved a

bullet, it didn't make it any easier for me to deliver it.

I placed the vodka bottle on the counter, then headed for the door. 'I'm out.'

'I know you feel that way,' he said. 'Unfortunately, things aren't that simple.'

'This is.'

'I told you when you joined… if you do, you're in it for the long haul.'

'I didn't know I'd be doing this!'

'We're in fluid situations. You need to be prepared for everything.'

He paused a moment, then took a deep breath. His tone softened. 'You're a valuable agent, Michael, and you'll only become more so. Give it time. It gets easier.'

'I don't want it to get easier! I don't want to end up some dead-eyed fuck who kills to pay the bills! I've seen these guys of yours, they're ghosts!'

'Michael…'

'I don't give a shit.'

'I may run Southwest, but there are people I have to answer to as well. Believe me, it's not as simple as you coming here and telling me that you're out. You're a criminal, Michael.'

'Was!'

'Nonetheless, there are plenty at Southwest who disagree with my employing agents with your background. You represent a significant risk to us. We've shared delicate information with you, information that could compromise us. I hate to say it, but it's not entirely down to me what might happen if you leave now.'

I went still. Just stared at him. I don't know why I found it so hard to believe that he'd threaten me, but I did.

He sighed to himself. 'Last year we were working with this talented young hacker. Bright boy, he'd been running banking scams for a couple of years before we caught him. We gave him the option to work for us. Two months ago, he decided he wanted to leave... threatened to go to the press if we didn't let him go. He died in police custody. Suicide, apparently, but I'm not exactly sure what happened.'

Motherfuckers. 'You guys are as bad as the people you target, you know that?'

'Honor never won a war, Michael, just ask any honorable government you can find.'

He shook his head, then wheeled himself back over to the cutlery drawer and started cutting up his sandwich.

'So,' he said. 'This is the world we're in. It's not just for your own good, it's for everybody's. Try to remember that.'

'You're not listening to me. I can't do it any more.'

'I'm going to have to disagree with you on that too, I'm afraid.'

He tapped at the LED screen – it flickered back into life.

'We have a job that's come in from Phoenix,' he said.

'I'm going home.'

He eyed me carefully for a moment. 'Yes,' he said.

'You're tired. I'll have the details sent to you.'

The bitterness in my eyes as I held his look.

'It's not urgent,' he said. 'But we'll need it done by the end of next week.'

Need it done? He was talking like my transition into hitman was already stamped and sealed.

I didn't know what to say. It felt like I was drowning, like my voice just didn't matter any more.

'Go home and rest,' he said.

The weight of it bearing down on me. I'd been railroaded. Cornered. No choice, and I hadn't even realized it.

I felt sick as I flew back to San Francisco that night. I gazed out of the window and listened to the murmur of the passengers around me. The sounds of normal lives. A family sitting across the aisle from me. The father was in his forties – a doctor by the sound of it – traveling with his petite wife and his pale, frightened-looking children. He kept talking about some medical conference he was going to attend. Which tie he should wear – whether the Oxford blue was too casual. Talking about the family's holiday plans to Toronto next month. About his lawn. His feet. About his sister in Maine and her favorite episode of *Gilmore Girls*. He kept droning on – I swear, his coma patients would wake up just so they could switch off their own life support. But I envied him. The life he had. Because what was I looking at now? A life spent waiting for strangers to arrive, shooting them dead, then biding my time until the next job. The life of a hitman wasn't glory and adventure. It was small and ugly and gray. A soulless job for people who had no business having anybody in their lives to care for. And all of a sudden holidays in Toronto and Oxford blue ties sounded like poetry. Shit, even *Gilmore Girls* would have felt like a meaning to life.

Yeah, they'd kill me. But they'd have to find me.

I'd take my chances.

I'd run.

It was sunrise when the cab took me into the city, the sky glowing gray above the Victorian walk-ups in the Mission. As the cab hushed through the empty streets, I tried to get my head straight. I'd need to move fast. It wouldn't be long before Arlen shared my visit with his superiors in DC – he'd have to. One of his criminal assets was a flight risk. Fuck, I shouldn't have told him anything.

I needed to get out of the country. I had a fake passport in my apartment that had no connection to Southwest. Some cash under the floorboards beneath my bed. I'd take the bus to Montreal, then fly out from there. I couldn't use a domestic airport – Southwest was plugged into the facial recognition system that the government used on airport surveillance cameras. The system didn't work half the time, but it wasn't a risk I needed to take.

The cab pulled up outside my apartment. I paid the driver, then headed for the dusty stone entrance to the building, the early morning streets still quiet around me. I grabbed my keys – then slowed a second. I stepped back from the door and stared down the side street by the building.

As a pickpocket, I'd spent most of my career lifting the keys to luxury cars. You do that long enough and you find yourself automatically clocking any interesting vehicles around you whether you're looking to steal them or not. A navy blue 1968 Mustang was parked in the side street beside my building. It was rare – but what really interested me about it was I knew Willard owned one.

I looked around. He'd never once visited me in San Francisco. He may have managed me at the agency, but we weren't exactly friends to say the least. I headed over to the Mustang and peered in through the windshield, looking for any sign it was his. It had California plates, but I couldn't remember Willard's registration. I looked for anything inside that I might recognize. Sunglasses or bags on the seats. The car was empty. Spotless. Cleaned to showroom perfection – but that was Willard all over.

I stared uneasily back at my apartment building. I didn't want to get paranoid, but I didn't want to take any chances either. I didn't like it that he was here. Then again, he'd parked the car in full view of my building, and he was well aware that I knew he owned one. He was probably here at Arlen's request to try and talk some sense into me. He'd probably tried to call, but after Massa's house had turned to crap, I'd dumped the phone.

Fine. I'd act like I'd cooled down. Like everything had settled.

I headed over to my building and quietly opened the main door. The light in the tiny hallway automatically flickered into life. I peered up the cramped staircase, then made my way up. Six in the morning, and I could hear the neighbors stirring in the building. I reached my landing, the narrow corridor empty and silent. I eased up a little and headed for my apartment – maybe the car wasn't his. As I reached my door, I heard noises from the apartment opposite mine. I listened for a second, but it was just Ronnie, getting ready for work. I slipped the key into the lock.

'Good morning,' came Willard's voice from behind me.

I turned to find him calmly stepping off the staircase that led up to the fourth floor. He'd probably been sitting up there, waiting – but it concerned me that he'd stayed out of sight.

'What are you doing here?' I said.

'I need to talk to you.'

He strolled toward me, a black briefcase in his left hand. I glanced at the fold in the upper left panel of his jacket. He was carrying a weapon, but Willard always did. I tried to read what was going on in his eyes, but that was a hard thing to do with him. In his late thirties, he had this sterile, colorless demeanor that matched everything else about him. Perfectly combed hair. Plain charcoal suit. White shirt buttoned up to the collar. No tie. Jesus, what the hell was he doing with a Mustang, he looked like an Amish Nascar driver.

'So talk,' I said.

'Can we go inside, please?'

He glanced back down the hallway like he was checking that we were alone. I felt the nerves rise in me – fear that some decision about me had already been made.

I stared carefully at him. 'You speak to Arlen?'

He nodded.

I opened the door and headed inside. As he followed me in, I eyed the living room window. There was a fire escape just outside, but the window was locked, I wouldn't have the time to open it. I glanced at the oak coffee table by the sofa – I had a gun taped to the bottom of it. As I tried to picture the exact position of the gun, Willard cleared a couple of magazines from the sofa, then sat down. He calmly unbuttoned his jacket and made himself comfortable.

'I tried to call,' he said.

I shrugged. 'Phone's at the bottom of Lake Michigan.'

He nodded, then glanced distastefully around the disheveled room.

'Arlen told me about your visit last night,' he said.

'Yeah?'

'It was stupid of you.'

'No argument there.'

He sighed, then brushed a few specks of dust from his suit. I glanced at the coffee table – he was sitting too close to it for me to make a move.

I gestured toward the kitchen. 'You want a drink? There's water in the fridge. Juice, I think.'

He smiled. 'You're not going to get it for me? A guest in your home?'

24

'Sure. If you want.'

'Water, please.'

I opened the fridge, poured him a glass, then headed back into the living room and handed it to him. He held the glass up to the light, checking to see it was clean. It evidently wasn't. He pushed the glass away onto the coffee table, then kept his eyes on me for a moment. He glanced around the room, briefly studying every piece of furniture.

His eyes returned to the coffee table.

'This where you keep your gun?' he said.

He reached an arm under the table top, felt around, then tore away the 9mm pistol taped to the underside. He carefully peeled the tape away from the gun, checked the clip, then snapped it back in.

I held my breath as he pointed it at me. Fuck.

He gazed keenly down the sight, then nodded.

'It's filthy,' he said. 'You need to clean it.'

He threw it to me.

'Relax,' he said. 'You'd be dead already.'

I breathed again, but didn't feel that much better that he was in my apartment.

'I'm actually here to help you,' he said.

I eyed him carefully.

'Please,' he said. 'Sit down.'

I slowly pulled up a chair, but kept hold of the gun.

He took a deep breath as he brushed away the folds in his jacket. 'It's no secret that I think your kind are a bad fit for the agency,' he said.

'My kind?'

'You have poor attitudes. Then again, that's what

you get when you hire criminals.'

I stayed quiet.

'Some things aren't going to change for you now, no matter what,' he said. 'You discuss us with anybody and you'll be dead long before Arlen needs to answer questions at a committee hearing.'

'He made that crystal clear to me, alright, so…'

'But the truth is, I'd be more than happy for you to leave. For you to just go.'

I searched his lifeless blue eyes.

'I'm here to offer you a deal,' he said. 'One more assignment for the agency, then you're out.'

'A hit?'

He nodded.

My heart sank at the thought of it.

'Arlen didn't seem to think that out was an option,' I said.

'Your kind have left before. But you leave on our terms, not yours.'

I kept my eyes on him. 'Who's the target?'

'Lenny Tripps.'

I'd heard of him – some big drug trafficker in Miami. Willard opened his briefcase, took out a yellow document file, then placed it on the table.

'Twice we've tried to hit him,' he said. 'Both attempts failed. He's a nasty little snake, slippery with it. You'll need to be careful.'

'Does Arlen know about this deal?'

He shook his head. 'He may run Southwest, but I manage the field. If I recommend discharging you, it'll happen.'

I laughed. 'I just take your word on that, do I?'

'I'll make sure you're out, Michael, don't worry. I don't want you working for us any more than you do. This is in both our interests.'

'Then discharge me now.'

'I need this first.'

He neatly adjusted the yellow folder so its corners were in line with the table.

'Arlen's not going to be running things for much longer,' he said. 'He can't. I'm one of three agents that DC are considering as the new director.'

'You?'

He nodded. 'But there's a mark against me. The Lenny Tripps job was my responsibility. I can't afford another failure.'

He pushed the file toward me.

'You have my word,' he said. 'You do this for me, and I'll cut you loose. You're a free man.'

I gazed at him.

Free. The word sounded like magic.

I sat out on the fire escape, the yellow folder beside me as I sipped at a chipped glass full of whiskey. My gaze fixed on the skyline, I tried to stay positive. I may not have wanted to kill any more, but if I had to, then a guy like Lenny Tripps would probably be high up on the list. A Miami drug lord, it wouldn't be hard to argue that I'd be doing the world a favor. These were the risks of his profession, territory he'd know well. Plus he had no family – no one to mourn his passing, which just made the whole business that much easier to consider. I nodded to myself. Yeah. This could be a way out for me. Assuming I could kill him, of course, which was a big assumption. I'd read the file – forty pages of photographs, surveillance and analysis – and with every page I'd turned, Willard's promise of freedom seemed to fade further away. If anything, going after Lenny Tripps was about as sure a way for me to get killed as running from the agency.

Officially, Lenny Tripps is in the tinned tuna business. He's done very well from it and is worth an estimated three billion dollars. *Forbes Magazine* listed him as 2017's 'Face of modern fish products', but they were just making a point. Lenny does own a tuna packing plant near Port of Savannah, but he's also the main distributor of Colombian cocaine to Florida and the east coast.

At the age of fifty-one, he's been the king of the Miami drugs scene for eight years now, and is largely credited for the city's recent resurgence as the drug trafficker's port of choice. Not that you'd know it to look at him. Unlike his Armani-clad contemporaries, Lenny Tripps is a Hawaiian shirt-wearing bulldog who doesn't care much for elegance. Three hundred pounds and hairy as a bear, he looks like someone built a snowman out of grease, then rolled it across a barbershop floor.

As brash as he is, he's nonetheless a very popular figure in the wider Miami population – he's like a local hero down there. Whenever he's interviewed, he gets huge ratings. Whenever there's killings in the city, there's huge crowds waiting to defend him to the press.

You can even buy T-shirts of the guy. The reason for this is simple: he may be the biggest trafficker on the east coast, but he's also a man of the people.

Over the years, Lenny has spent hundreds of millions of dollars building schools and hospitals across southern Florida. Barwell House, a medical facility that treats children from underprivileged backgrounds, is financed almost entirely by Lenny – as is Rykers Hospital in Fort Lauderdale. Last year alone he flew nineteen children and their families to Israel for experimental radiotherapy. This kind of involvement in public life has seen Lenny Tripps rise to the level of saint in Florida's poorer communities. Of course there are plenty who maintain that Lenny's passion for philanthropy is simply a passion for good PR – and they may be right. But he's doing it well. People love him, and as a result there's very little political pressure to go after him. It almost seemed like a shame to put a bullet in the guy.

It's not just politicians who've turned a blind eye to Lenny, either – the police are remarkably tolerant of him too. There are two reasons for this. Firstly, he pays them off. But secondly, and perhaps more importantly, so long as drug dealers are killing each other, no one really gives a crap. If you go into the drug business, you know full well you're entering a violent world – no one's going to shed a tear for you if you end up dead. It's not like you went into the greeting card business and the guys from Hallmark blew up your car. No matter what war Lenny may be waging, he always takes great care to make sure his beloved public doesn't get hurt – and it's made him a very popular figure in the process. The authorities may not be happy he's running Miami, but someone's going to run it, and it's better the devil you know. On the demonic scale, Lenny is definitely at the acceptable end.

At least, he was.

Five months ago that all changed. A bomb at a ski cabin in Oregon killed nine people, none of whom had anything to do with the drug business. Among the victims were three children. It marked the end of Lenny's paternal attitude.

The main target of the bombing was a Miami businessman named Will Jerome. A real estate developer and Congressional candidate, Will was a hugely outspoken opponent of Lenny's. He refused to be taken in by the PR machine and regularly called Lenny out for what he was – a drug-peddling curse on the city. In one very public confrontation he had with Lenny, Will took a TV crew to the apartment building where Lenny lives. Never one to shy away from the cameras, Lenny met him in the lobby and defended himself against Will's accusations.

'Cocaine destroys lives,' said Will.

'I don't know much about that,' replied Lenny. 'I'd say alcohol probably destroys a hell of a lot more lives though. It seems the only people who have a problem with cocaine are the ones who aren't making any money off of it.'

'Not like you.'

'I'm a legitimate businessman, Will.'

'You're a killer. The largest distributor of cocaine in

Florida. You're a shark.'

'That's funny,' said Lenny. 'You know how many people died of shark attacks last year? Four. You know how many died falling off chairs? Six. Not only is your information about me wrong, your analogies are for shit too.'

As Lenny walked off, Will started reading out the names and ages of all the Miami citizens who'd died as a result of drug abuse that past year. It took him twenty minutes.

The lobby interview turned out to be the last confrontation Will would have with Lenny. In a bid to undermine Lenny's increasing grip on the city, Will launched a campaign to stop Lenny from attaining a majority shareholding in a real estate development in South Miami. Will's campaign was a success and he managed to stop the sale of the shares. Lenny lost nearly thirty million dollars in the process. Six weeks later, Will was on a skiing holiday with friends when twenty pounds of C-4 blew the cabin they were in to shit. It wasn't just a hit – it was rage. A family from a neighboring cabin had been visiting at the time – among them were three children. While there's little doubt Lenny was unaware the family was there, the fact that he'd kill so indiscriminately marked a dramatic change in his style – and an equally dramatic change in the public's attitude toward him. Three children died, and a lot of the goodwill that Lenny enjoyed burned up along with them.

The Oregon bombing has signaled the end for Lenny. He's fallen into the same filthy bucket as every other drug boss, and the authorities aren't making dispensations for him any more. In the five months since the bombing, the police have been going after him – shutting down his operations wherever they can find them and generally making life as hard as they can for his associates. They arrested him for the bombing, but couldn't hold him – all they had was a motive and word on the street that it was Lenny who did it. But without a single person willing to testify, Lenny is currently a free man.

Although hopes of finding evidence linking Lenny to the bombing have started to fade, the desire to see him held accountable hasn't. Will Jerome was a popular figure in Florida – in DC, too. Conversations have evidently taken place in quiet rooms, with orders passed down the chain until word finally reached Southwest. Lenny Tripps has to pay. In one respect it's an easy option for the decision makers in DC. When a drug trafficker dies, all suspicions turn toward the trafficker's competitors. The problematic part is how you actually kill him. Lenny has made that a very hard thing to do.

Being a drug lord will make you rich, but it'll also make you the biggest target in town. Lenny has plenty of ambitious competitors who'd love to put a bullet in him, and his world has shrunk dramatically as a result. Four years ago he completed construction of a luxury condo in Coconut Grove – the unimaginatively titled 'Sunset Marina'. The condo has moorings for a hundred and twenty boats, and apartments that overlook Biscayne Bay. The apartments start at two million dollars, and Lenny would have made a lot of money if he'd sold any of them. The problem is he moved into the penthouse, and with the number of people who want him dead, no one wants to live anywhere near him. Sunset Marina is largely empty as a result. The upside for Lenny is that, with his men now renting the lower apartments, the marina has inadvertently become his own personal fortress. There was an attack on the building last year by the Lonos gang – twelve guys. They didn't even make it past the lobby.

Which brings us the main difficulty when trying to get Lenny. You'd have thought that the Lonos gang would have waited until Lenny left the building and hit him on the street. Problem: Lenny never leaves the building.

With the number of enemies he's made, Lenny has become this Howard Hughes-style recluse. He's developed a phobia of being on the ground in recent years, and is never seen on street level any more. He has another equally well-guarded penthouse just up the coast that he occasionally visits by helicopter, but that's about it – two apartments and a helicopter are Lenny's entire world at the moment. In an interview he gave to the *Miami Herald*, he explained that, 'The ground's a shitty fucking place. Ninety-two per cent of all shootings, ninety-four per cent of stabbings, and ninety-nine per cent of all car accidents take place at ground level. Live in the air, only travel by air, to other places that are in the air.'

The reporter then asked him, 'What about

helicopter crashes?'

Lenny shrugged. 'It's the ground that gets them every time.'

This kind of paranoia has made Lenny a hard target – and not just for his competitors, for Southwest too. Willard sent in two agents before me. One rented a sailboat, moored it by the tower, then promptly disappeared. No one has heard from him since. The second suggested that a missile strike on Lenny's helicopter would be the best way forward. However, the collateral damage of it crashing into the streets below was deemed too costly. Even if they could hit it over the sea, Lenny's helicopter was fitted with decoy flares, making a successful strike unlikely. Instead, the agent took a sniper shot at Lenny as he crossed the rooftop toward the helicopter pad. He missed. Now Lenny has bulletproof glass lining the walkway that leads from the roof exit to the pad. About the only thing you could hope for is that he gets struck down by an act of God, but I bet he's got smite-proof glass everywhere too.

A reclusive king sitting in his tower, Lenny has been hidden away for nearly four years now, guarded by a loyal army of lieutenants and foot soldiers who handle everything for him. Which would explain why Willard had given the job to me.

If Lenny never comes out, then someone was going to have to go in.

3

I sat on the deck of the power boat, the heat hammering down as I swayed in the waves off Coconut Grove. The sunlight flared across the water like it was bouncing off a blade. I loosened the baseball cap against my sweating head, then gazed again at the photographs on my phone.

The youngest of the Oregon bombing victims was four years old: Lucy Hocroft, a shy-looking girl with wispy blonde hair and huge, searching green eyes. The ferocious nature of her death itched away at me as I slowly flipped through the other photos. Images of Lucy's brother and sister. Of their parents. Of Will Jerome. Of the married couple who'd owned the cabin, friends of Will's. Willard had sent me the photos in a bid to make sure that I saw this through, and it was working.

It wasn't hard summoning up the will to kill Lenny Tripps.

'You OK?' said Murray.

I nodded, then draped the fishing rod back over the stern of the boat.

It was Murray's boat. He ran fishing trips – cheap ones. In his forties and a real mess with it, his clothes were covered in chocolate crumbs and potato chips. He looked like the victim of a drive-by snacking.

He smiled. 'Not doing too good here, huh?'

I shrugged. I hadn't caught a thing.

'It's your money,' he said. 'But I'm telling you, we need to go further out.'

'It's fine, I'm good.'

I waved the fishing line around in the water like I had any idea what I was doing, and kept my eyes on Sunset Marina.

I'd been in Miami a week now. The first six days I'd spent holed up in a room at the Grand that had a view of the inland side of the Marina. Six days and not a single clue how I was going to get in. I'd come out on the boat, trying to get a measure of the ocean side. But there was no joy here either.

I gazed at the Marina tower – a glass cylinder that rose fourteen floors above the palms and yacht masts that surrounded its base. It was built on an artificial outcrop that stretched three hundred and fifty feet out into the sea, which meant the only way in was via the road that connected it to Palm Boulevard. The tower itself may have stood out, but there was little detail to be seen inside. The building's glass was smoked a deep green and had a mirror-like quality to it. Even with binoculars you couldn't see much. The only decent view inside was at the main entrance. Not that it was a particularly pleasant sight – the lobby was pure Egyptian-styled glitz. Marble pillars covered in hieroglyphs and rhinestones. A glass plinth resting between two stone sphinxes that served as the reception desk. Gold leaf on every surface. It looked like the last delirious throes of Cleopatra, like she'd tried to design a condo while dying of snake bite.

But it was the security that went with it. The government spends one point five billion dollars a year on Presidential security. Lenny was worth twice that, and it looked like he was spending every cent of it on guards, scanners, and metal detectors. In six days, I hadn't seen a single person enter the tower without at least two of the eight guards who continually patrolled the lobby, searching and scanning them before escorting them in.

It's not like there were any other viable entrances. There was a rear exit on the ocean side, which had been the first thing I'd looked at when I came out in Murray's boat. But that exit had three guards – even if you got by them, you'd just find yourself back in the lobby having to deal with the other eight. You could climb in, maybe, from one of the apartment balconies. But the lower balconies were sealed with storm shutters, and it had to be a hundred-foot climb to the first open one. Not that climbing was particularly inviting anyway – if I got caught on my way up, I'd be a sitting duck. No, I was going to have to walk in through the front door like a regular person.

I shook my head to myself, then tossed the fishing rod onto the deck. The heat and frustration were gnawing at me. I'd spent a week stalking Lenny's building like some lone wolf, but for all the threat I posed to him right now, I might as well have been a carrot that was stalking him.

As I bathed in the sun for a moment, my phone

rang.

It was Willard. Shit.

I glanced back at Murray. 'You got any more beer?'

As he headed down into the boat, I answered the call.

'Yeah.'

'Update, please,' said Willard.

'The fishing didn't help.'

'What now?'

'I don't have a what now, I'm just going to have to wait and see.'

'I've told DC you're on the job. They're expecting results.'

I gazed again at the tower. 'You got any other information you can send me? Anything, it doesn't matter.'

'Everything's in the file.'

I sighed heavily.

'You get the photographs?' he said.

'Yeah.'

I thought to myself a moment – it seemed like a small thing. 'Although, there were nine victims. You only sent eight photos.'

'One of the victims still hasn't been identified. A female in her early twenties.'

'A friend of Will's maybe?'

'We don't know. There's been no missing persons reports that match her.'

I tried to get a handle on this. Nine times out of ten, no missing persons reports meant the victim was either a drug addict or a prostitute. Will Jerome would have been the only guy at the cabin that afternoon who didn't have a wife in tow – but he didn't strike me as the kind of guy who'd have hired company like that.

Willard muttered impatiently, 'Alright, stay focused. I want news tomorrow.'

I nodded. 'Yeah.'

But I didn't hold out much hope of that. I was getting nowhere here. I hung up, grabbed the lifeless fishing rod, then once again turned my attention back to Sunset Marina.

I got back to the hotel at about eight that night. I took one look at the Marina tower looming outside my window, then went straight back out again. Eighteen hours a day watching that place – it was frying my head. I needed music and female company, even if it was just for a few hours.

I strolled through the bustling streets of Coconut Grove. The gentle roar of the ocean in the distance, the palm trees shivering in the evening breeze. As I scanned the clubs and bars, looking for a place to hang for a while, I caught sight of a pink glow down one of the side streets. A club called The Pepper Bar. The place looked good – a Lamborghini Aventador parked outside. Not that you'll ever meet a guy in a Lamborghini who you'll like, but there's always crowds of pretty and, more importantly, desperate girls around them.

I headed down into the club, the neon depths glowing like a nuclear reactor. I squeezed over to the bar, ordered a double Scotch, then gazed at the crowds – a sweating mass of bleached hair and glitter. Seventies disco streaming from the speakers. I took a large mouthful of the Scotch, then stared at the dance floor. A group of girls heading down the white marble steps toward it. One of them glanced at me – a glossy-haired brunette in her twenties. A quiet confidence about her, I kept my eyes on her as she started to dance. She smiled at me. I took another mouthful of Scotch and weaved my way toward her. I reached the dance floor – then slowed a second. The sound of a man's voice ringing out above the crowds behind me.

'Michael! Michael!'

As I gazed at the silhouettes, a figure emerged into the pink light. A guy in his mid-thirties wearing a shiny black tracksuit. Slicked black hair. Dark, sunken eyes. Shit, I recognized him. Danny Perino. He'd worked for a hood in San Francisco that I used to steal cars for.

'Michael, what the fuck are you doing here!'

'Danny!' I said.

He looked stoned out of his skull as he stumbled over and threw his arms around me.

'It's good to see you!' he said.

I hid my disappointment at running into him. 'You too.'

'Jesus,' he said. 'What's it been, four, five years?'

'Something like that.'

'Man, just look at you!'

The sweat on his face as he laughed – a giggle like a small child's.

'So what's up?' he said. 'Still working for Berry?'

40

I shook my head. 'Not for a while.'

'Me neither. I'm down here now. Doing great.' He lowered his voice. 'You still lifting keys?'

I shrugged. 'A little.'

'I fucking bet, man! You were, like, totally good!'

I glanced at the brunette on the dance floor – she smiled at me again. She was definitely the preferable option to hanging with Danny.

'Look, it's good seeing you,' I said to him. 'We should definitely get together.'

As I turned and headed for the dance floor, he grabbed me by the arm.

'No, no, we need to talk,' he said. 'I can't fucking believe this!'

'I'll give you my number. Call me tomorrow.'

'No, no, now,' he said.

I sighed wearily as he started dragging me through the crowds toward an anonymous door in one corner of the club. I was too tired to argue with him – I'd give him five minutes, then head back to the brunette. As we approached the door, a thick-necked heavy standing guard opened it for us. On the other side was a small private room – white LED screens covering the walls, ceiling to floor. Some stoned guy and his half-naked girlfriend were draped across a circular sofa.

Danny nodded at them. 'Get out.'

No argument. They grabbed the girl's clothes and scrambled to their feet, the two of them glancing to see who I was as Danny ushered them out of the room.

Danny closed the door, the music fading to a dull thud. On the table in the middle of the sofa sat two champagne buckets. Danny grabbed one of the bottles.

'Champagne?' he said.

I raised my Scotch. 'I'm good.'

He poured himself a glass, then invited me to sit.

'So who are you working for now?' he said.

'Me, mostly.'

'Still doing cars?'

'Uh-huh.'

'That's good. That's why you're in Miami?'

I nodded. 'I've got a little something going on.'

He giggled. 'Little something going on. I fucking love you, man.'

He took a mouthful of champagne, then winked at me.

'So what you driving?' he said. 'Still got the Aston?'

I shook my head. 'Couldn't be bothered with it any more.'

'You're kidding, I loved that car.' He smiled, then pointed at his chest. 'Lamborghini Aventador.'

'That's yours? I saw it.'

He giggled again. 'You keep your hands off it too. Fucking girls love it, man. This one I met last week, you wouldn't believe her. She's just like... yeah! Fucking ass in my face. Just... fucking yeah!'

'No, she sounds lovely.'

'That's the word. She's like art, man... it's like you're literally fucking a painting.'

I really didn't have the energy for this, but I raised a polite smile anyhow. 'It sounds like you're doing well, Danny.'

'Yeah, yeah, get this.'

He took another huge mouthful of champagne, the wine dripping down the front of his tracksuit as he sat opposite me. 'You know who I work for now?' He flashed his eyes. 'Emilio Lonos.'

I stared blankly at him, but I'd heard of Lonos from Lenny's file. It was Lonos' gang who'd attacked the Marina last year and got their asses kicked. The guy was a psycho by all accounts – a man whose attraction to oblivion had seen him rise to the silver medal position in Miami's crime scene in just a few short years.

Danny nodded. 'Emilio runs Miami, man. You should come work for him. I'm fucking serious. He could really use a guy with your hands.'

I paused for a moment, then took a sip of Scotch.

'I thought Lenny Tripps was the guy down here,' I said.

'Fuck Lenny! He's finished!'

'That's not what I've heard.'

'He's done, man. Fucking rock n' roll. The city's ours.'

I eyed him carefully. 'Why, you guys waging war on him or something?'

He giggled. 'No, no. Not us.'

He leaned right across the table, then lowered his voice. 'There's been some outside talent in town the past few months. Not sure who, but Emilio thinks it's government.'

I went still. 'Why does he think that?'

'Word is Tripps' guys caught one of them by the

43

marina. Fucking tattoos, some ex-military creep. Stinks of government, man.' He nodded. 'They're bringing him down.'

He caught his breath, then wiped the champagne from his mouth. 'Anyhow, Emilio's got work for you. No cars. I'm talking real work, real money.'

'Doing what?'

'Keys, man! You can get in anywhere. Fucking judges, police chiefs… we're gonna rule!' He started slapping at the table. 'You're the man, Michael! I'm going to bring you to Emilio.' He jumped to his feet. 'Come on, he's at the Palace.'

'I can't right now.'

'No, no, now!'

'I can't, Danny.'

His mood shifted gear like a spoiled five-year-old. He grabbed me by the arm. 'Let's go!'

I stayed firm. 'Danny.'

The heat in his eyes as I gently grabbed his hand and removed it from my arm.

'Fuck this!' he said.

'Danny… Danny!' I needed to calm this idiot down. 'There's a Ferrari California at the Hyatt. The guy who owns it is in this bar. I'm getting twenty-five if I can deliver it to the docks by midnight tonight, OK?'

He blinked heavily, then nodded – the anger in him ebbing away as fast as it had risen.

'Yeah,' he said. 'Yeah, alright.' He looked lost for a second, his shoulders twitching slightly.

He threw his arms around me again. 'It's fucking good to see you, man.'

I rolled my eyes. 'Yeah. You too.'

'Give me your number,' he said.

He took out his phone, and I gave him a fake number.

'We'll speak soon,' I said.

'Yeah. Yeah, Emilio's going to love you, man.'

I headed back out into the bar and sighed wearily. I weaved through the crowds, looking for the brunette, but I couldn't find her now. Not that it mattered – running into Danny had killed my mood. It had always been a fair assumption that Lenny knew the government was gunning for him, but the fact that a relative nobody like Danny Perino knew about it too made me feel less like a covert agent and more like a public executioner.

I trudged back toward the hotel, tired of the heat, the people and everything else to do with this job. I crossed the Boulevard and headed for the hotel's main entrance. As I did, a red Mini Cooper blared its horn as it zipped past, nearly clipping me. I jumped back onto the sidewalk and took a deep breath. Shit, I really was tired. The Mini slowed as it approached the intersection. For a moment it looked like the driver was going to get out and yell at me, but no one appeared – the car just waited for the traffic to clear. I eyed it curiously as it then turned left into the darkness of the Marina Road and headed for the tower. I stepped toward the intersection and took a closer look. I hadn't seen it here before.

Three of the tower guards approached the car as it pulled up by the main entrance. They seemed calm about the arrival, they were evidently expecting it. The car doors opened and two figures got out – a man and a woman. The woman was in her late twenties, wearing army fatigue pants and a white vest. I'd seen her before, she'd visited last Tuesday evening. Monroe-styled, platinum bleached hair. Tattoos all over her arms. Pretty, if you like that kind of thing. The guy traveling with her was new though. In his early thirties, short black Mohican, he looked twitchy as he grabbed a large, cube-shaped bag from the back of the Mini. He swung it over his shoulder and followed the woman into the lobby, eyeing her nervously as the guards ushered the two of them into a room just beyond the reception desk. On Tuesday, the woman had remained in the room for ten minutes, where she was no doubt thoroughly searched, before being escorted into an elevator. It looked like the same routine this evening. I stepped under a thick row of palm trees on the Boulevard and waited. The woman had arrived by cab on Tuesday, but not tonight. I noted down the license plate of the Mini, then turned over the possibilities of what might be in the bag. It looked heavy. But the arrival was too overt for cash or drugs. Weapons, maybe, but there had to be a huge armory in the tower already. Unless she was some hooker, and the bag contained fetish gear or something. Maybe the guy was, too. You never know what Lenny might be into.

Ten minutes later, the two of them exited the room and were escorted across the lobby. The moment they disappeared into the elevator, one of the lobby guards headed out to the Mini. He checked under the hood, took a look in the trunk, then extended a telescopic mirror and checked underneath the car. Whoever this woman was, Lenny didn't trust her either. The guard then climbed inside the car and drove it toward the glowing concrete mouth that led to the Tower's underground parking lot. I grabbed my keys. I'd missed the woman leaving on the Tuesday, but I wouldn't tonight. I headed across the street to the hotel parking lot and got into my rented BMW. I pulled out onto the Boulevard, parked a couple of hundred feet from the intersection, and waited again.

It was nearly an hour before the Mini pulled back out onto the Boulevard. I switched off the radio and carefully eyed the car. The same man and woman in it – the woman driving. I started up the BMW and tailed them as they headed south.

Saturday night and the Grove was a sweating blur of silhouettes and pink neon. The tourists spilling off the sidewalk kept the traffic at a crawl and made the Mini easy to follow. The car wound through the crowds for about a mile, then hit the highway. I kept three or four cars behind them as the highway started to climb. The lights of the coast glittered in the distance as an overpass took us high across the city, past the glowing office buildings and billboards, and then down into the deep green shadows of Coral Gables.

The Gables was a little designer jungle. Boutiques nestled in Spanish archways, the whole area thick with trees. The Mini continued south for a few minutes, then slowed in the middle of the road ahead of me. I calmly passed the car, keeping my eyes on it in the rearview mirror. The car turned off the road and disappeared down a backstreet. I swung the BMW around, switched off the headlights, then crawled into the backstreet after them. The Mini's lights were way ahead of me as it weaved between the dumpsters and fire escapes. The glow then ground to a halt. I stopped the BMW accordingly. I couldn't see much at the far end of the backstreet, just the vaguest sense of movement as the guy took the bag from the rear seats. From the sluggish way he was moving, the bag seemed as heavy as it had been when he'd arrived at the tower.

The guy followed the woman down a narrow alleyway. I got out of the car and crept after them, ducking between the pools of sodium light that hung over the fire escapes. I neared the alleyway, then angled my approach to get a better view. They'd disappeared. Shit. I glanced around, then darted down the alleyway, keeping myself tight against the walls. A filthy little courtyard appeared just ahead of me. Rotting scraps of food and cigarette butts. Rows of garbage cans sitting beside the black lacquered rear door of one of the buildings. Beyond them, a concrete staircase led up to the units above – a row of offices by the look of it. As I stepped toward the staircase, the black lacquered door swung open. A sweaty guy in an apron dumped a garbage bag by the door. He eyed me for a moment, then headed back inside. As the door swung closed behind him, I went still – a glimpse of a bustling restaurant kitchen beyond the door. And standing in the middle of it was the tattooed woman. I reached for the door and pulled it open a fraction – watching as the woman took a sip of wine and buttoned herself into a brilliant white cotton smock.

She was no hooker, she was a chef.

A man's voice from somewhere in the kitchen. 'All good?'

The woman nodded. 'Thirty-two guests confirmed. He's going with the Dover sole and the lamb.'

'How was Zack?'

She smiled. 'Nervous.'

'I bet he was. Lenny Tripps, are you kidding me?'

'It was fine. We're going to order some extra bottles… they liked the Malbec and the Burgundy.'

'The Burgundy? We won't get that in by tomorrow night.'

'I'll ask Ronnie, he's always got it.'

A figure zipped past the gap in the door – I stepped back into the shadows of the courtyard. I just stood there for a moment, trying to get my head straight. It sounded like she was catering a party at Lenny's. Why not? He may have been a paranoid recluse, but he'd want to be living his life even if he never left the building.

I approached the crack in the kitchen door again. I couldn't see the chef now, but I could hear her on her phone, talking to someone about the wine she needed for tomorrow night. A relaxed playfulness in her voice, like catering for the biggest hood on the east coast was just another night for her. As she ended the call, I kept close to the door and listened carefully. Nothing now but the bustle of the kitchen – orders and services, boiling pots and sizzling pans. I waited a little longer, then headed down the alleyway until I hit the main road. I stared at the restaurant's facade – the peach-lit, Spanish-styled entrance of 'Charivari'. I glanced inside; a dimly lit blend of the ancient and the modern. Rough rock and mortar walls that could have been from a monastery. But subtle high-tech lighting and dark, brushed steel tables – all of them full. The guy who'd accompanied the chef to Lenny's then appeared behind the bar at the far end, his Mohican like a strip of Velcro. He glanced at an order sheet, then started mixing drinks. I eyed him carefully. It seemed like he was the only bartender here – the guy who'd been covering for him, heading off and rejoining the waiters.

I nodded to myself. A party at Lenny's tomorrow – the chef catering – this guy handling the bar. Malbec and Burgundy. Any money there were sample wines in the bag he'd taken with him. There could be a way in for me here.

I pushed open the main door and stepped inside the restaurant. A skinny waiter with purple-dyed hair approached me.

'You have a reservation, sir?' he said.

'I'm just going to get a drink if that's OK.'

He ushered me in. African music floating through the buzz of conversations as I headed over to the bar and sat down.

The bartender nodded at me. 'What can I get you?'

'Vodka tonic, please. Grey Goose.'

He grabbed a glass, filled it with ice, then started pouring the measures. I kept my eyes on him as he did. Taking this guy's place was a definite possibility – I'd done plenty of bar work before. When I was starting out as a pickpocket, I spent six months serving drinks in the hotels around the Financial District, scouting the rich clientele and lifting their car keys. In the process I learned how to mix a whole barrel load of drinks. What's more, I could toss a slice of lemon into a glass from about six feet away pretty consistently. Although that had more to do with me being a thief who was just good with his hands, it gave me the air of bartender who had a little style and experience.

He placed the vodka tonic in front of me. 'That'll be twelve dollars.'

I handed him fifteen. 'Keep it.'

He nodded.

I took a sip of the vodka, then offered him a handshake. 'I'm Rick.'

'Zack,' he replied.

'It's a great place you've got here. I've heard a lot about it.'

He smiled.

'I'm looking for bar work,' I said. 'You got anything?'

'Afraid not. I know Ronnie's are looking for staff, you could try there. It's the next block up.'

I glanced around the restaurant – the waiters all nose rings, tattoos, and chopped, dyed hair. 'I don't know, I kind of like this place. It's got a different vibe to it.'

'Ronnie's are a little more conservative, but they're a decent bunch. You should give them a try.'

I shook my head. 'I'm done with conservative. I was at the White Room before this.'

He shot me a look. 'In DC?'

I nodded.

He looked impressed, and with good reason. The White Room was famous – a real high-class place. It was where DC's political elite hung out. I'd never been, but I knew Willard took meetings there sometimes. It was a good bet that either he or Arlen would know someone there who could arrange cover for me.

'Look, you don't even have to give me tips,' I said. 'First week I'll work for nothing. You don't want to keep me on after that, I'll leave, no problem.'

He raised his eyebrows. 'A week for nothing?'

I nodded. 'I need the change. I like it here.'

He stared thoughtfully at me.

'Alright, give me a moment,' he said.

He stepped out from the bar, headed toward the kitchen, then disappeared behind the door. I took another sip of the vodka and tried to think how this could work. Getting rid of Zack wouldn't be too much of a problem. I didn't want to do anything to hurt him, he seemed like a nice enough guy – but spike his coffee with a little eczema cream, and he'd be puking his guts up for the next forty-eight hours. Getting the chef to take me along as his replacement would be trickier though. She wouldn't take some guy she hardly knew into Lenny's home no matter how good a bartender I was. If I was going to get the gig, I'd need us to connect quickly, and to do that, I'd need personal information on her.

The kitchen door swung open and Zack reappeared with the chef. I eyed her carefully as she approached the bar. White cotton smock. Green cargo pants with a buttoned pocket in the flank of the right leg. Resting inside the pocket, the curved-cornered shape of a cellphone.

She sat beside me at the bar and shook my hand. 'I'm Alice,' she said.

'Rick,' I said. 'It's a pleasure.'

She leaned across the bar and grabbed an olive, gently chewing at it as she looked me up and down.

'The White Room,' she said. 'That's impressive.'

I shrugged modestly.

'How long were you there for?' she said.

'A little over three months. I'd have stayed longer, but it wasn't really for me.'

'Why's that?'

'It's just DC. All anyone ever talks about is money... like the only reason Man came down from the trees was because he dropped his wallet.'

She smiled.

'So what brings you all the way down here?' she said.

'Not much. Just traveling.'

'Just traveling?' She flashed her eyes. 'Searching for something or running from something?'

I smiled. 'A little of both.'

'Yeah? What are you running from?'

'Ah, nothing. Dad wants me to take over the business, but I'm not sure it's for me. Lawnmowers... the sale and repair of. Thrilling huh?'

She kept her eyes on me as she grabbed another olive and slipped it into her mouth. A breezy air about her, like she had all the time in the world to do whatever she wanted.

'OK, let's see what you've got,' she said. 'Make me a White Russian.'

I nodded. White Russian – ice, vodka, Kahlua and milk. A truly hideous creation. I got up from the bar stool, Alice following me as I headed round to Zack's side of the bar. I grabbed a tumbler, placed it on the bar, then reached into the ice bucket and started flicking cubes one by one toward the tumbler. A four-foot shot, they arced through the air, landing cleanly in the glass.

Alice smiled at me. 'They go for that at the White Room, do they?'

I shook my head.

No matter – my little circus act had landed cleanly enough to make an impression. I poured the Stolichnaya. Kahlua. Full-fat milk. I gave it a stir and slid it toward her.

She took a tiny sip, ran her tongue across her lips, then thought to herself a moment.

She eyed me carefully. 'One week, no tips?'

I nodded.

'OK, we'll start you at the lunch service on Monday,' she said.

That was no good to me. 'I'm free tomorrow if you

want. The sooner I start, the better.'

She raised her eyebrows. 'Keen.'

'That's me.'

She glanced at Zack a moment, then smiled.

'OK, I'll need you here by eleven,' she said. 'Bring your paperwork with you then.'

I nodded, then slid the Kahlua back onto the shelf. As I did, I glanced at the outline of her phone resting against the pocket fabric. Chances are it needed a fingerprint to unlock it.

'Let me give you my number anyhow,' I said. 'You got a phone?'

She unbuttoned her pocket and produced a silver iPhone 8. As she pressed her thumb against the home button, I glanced around the bar counter for a fragment of dirt or fluff. A tiny thread of discarded cotton on the counter – I pressed a fingertip against it and curled it into my palm.

I gave her the number. She keyed it in, then slipped the phone back in her pocket. I started counting down sixty seconds – the usual time it took an iPhone to lock itself.

'OK,' she said. 'Pleasure meeting you, Rick.'

'Likewise.'

I paused a moment, then stared at her.

I gestured toward her hair. 'You've got a little, er…' I pointed toward the platinum strands hanging down the side of her face. 'Something's caught in it.'

She brushed her hand through her hair.

I kept my eyes on her. 'No, it's still…' I gently raised my left hand. 'Do you mind?'

I brushed at the strands of hair. As I revealed the wispy thread of cotton to her, my right hand breezily unbuttoned her flank pocket – my middle and ring fingers slipping out her phone. I tapped the screen to restart the lock countdown, then slid it into my jeans. I brushed the cotton thread away from my fingertips.

'We're a proper little gentleman, aren't we,' she said.

'I have my moments.'

She smiled at me again. 'I'll see you tomorrow.'

As she turned and headed back toward the kitchen, Zack nodded at me.

'Welcome aboard,' he said.

'Thanks,' I replied.

I headed back round to the customer side of the bar. 'I'm just going to finish my drink, then I'll leave you guys to it.'

As Zack started mixing another drinks order, I took out Alice's phone and started scrolling through her apps. I didn't want to leave with it. She might get suspicious if the last time she remembered having it was around the new guy. But I didn't make too much of a deal about hiding it while I sat there – it could have been mine.

The first thing I noticed was she didn't have any kind of social media. No Facebook, Twitter, Instagram, nothing. A private person by the look of it, which was a shame – social media was a gold mine of personal details. Still, no matter. I opened her emails. I typed the word 'doctor' into the search bar, and waited. I'd always found that medical conditions were a great way of connecting with someone. I once pretended to have Huntsberger Syndrome in order to get close to the chairman of Barker Hardware. It was a great bonding experience. I managed to steal his uncle's Bugatti. A list of emails containing 'doctor' then appeared on the phone. I browsed a few, but they seemed to be mostly social emails from friends – none of them suggested that she had any medical conditions. I cleared the search, then typed in the word 'delivery' – shopping habits was another good one. A list of 'delivery date' emails filled the screen. A lot of books about astronomy. Star charts. *Merlin's Tour of the Universe* by Neil deGrasse Tyson. *Uncharted Galaxy* by Howard Lett. She even had a telescope delivered last April. I nodded to myself – I could use that. I continued scanning the delivery emails. A couple of iPads. A blender. A few books about cuisine, nothing new there. A few Star Wars toys – probably gifts. I slowed as a couple of orders then caught my eye. She'd bought two novels by an author named Zoy Rigby. I'd never heard of Rigby, but that was good, it was specific. I typed Zoy Rigby into the search bar, and got nine emails stretching back over the past four years – all of them purchases of novels. Alice was evidently a fan. I pulled up Google and did a search. It seems Rigby was a Canadian author whose work centered around themes of abandonment and loneliness. A reclusive writer who shunned publicity, she wasn't well known outside of her home country. Perfect.

I wouldn't say that I knew Alice – but I knew how

to lie to her, which was nearly as good. Zoy Rigby and astronomy. You don't need a symphony to serenade someone, just a few well-chosen notes. With no one ever remembering where they put their phone, I slipped it onto the bar, and headed out.

4

I didn't sleep that night. Nerves and doubts prickling at me. I might have finally found a way in to Lenny's, but all I could think about was how the hell I was going to get out. Killing him in the middle of a party was going to rapidly shrink my exit options. The guests were probably going to be his high-ranking men – killers, all of them. You add the marina guards to the mix, and the odds of me getting out of there alive definitely weren't tipping in my favor.

At 8:00 a.m. I called Willard and explained the situation at the restaurant. It was the first time I'd heard him sound excited by anything. Then again, he just wanted the hit checked off his list. I doubt he cared much whether I survived or not.

'You're sure the party's tonight?' he said.

'By the sound of it.'

'And you're close enough to the chef?'

'Not yet, but I will be.'

He thought to himself a moment.

'Alright,' he said. 'Alright, let's assume she takes you with her. You're not going to get a gun in there. How are you going to do it?'

It was a good question. One that I hadn't figured out a good answer to yet.

'Potassium cyanide is probably going to be your best option,' he said.

I shook my head. 'Not a chance.'

'If you're making him drinks…'

'Forget it.'

I'd already looked into poisons. It was too risky. Although the effects of cyanide are immediate, the victim can remain alive for anything up to three minutes. In that time Lenny would have to be an idiot not to know that I'd poisoned him and raise the alarm.

'What about something slower-acting?' I said. 'Give me time to get out.'

'Then there's the chance of him getting treatment.'

'That Russian guy in London, they poisoned him with radium or something.'

'If you think you're getting anything radioactive into that building, Michael. Just keep it simple. Use the knives in his kitchen.'

I sighed. 'Yeah.' But I kind of wanted to avoid that too. Lenny was a big guy. Unless I got it right, he might survive long enough to raise the alarm, and once again I'd be fucked. I needed something simple and immediate when he and I were alone – then hide the body long enough for me to get out. I really needed to get a gun in there.

I stared at the photo of Lenny in his file, his huge face staring back at me. Willard began muttering something about self-assembly plastic pistols, but even if I got them through the metal detectors, I had to count on being full-body searched. I went still as a detail in Lenny's file then caught my attention – the first piece of information written beneath his photograph. His date of birth.

'The party,' I said. 'It's his birthday.'

I paused and stared carefully at the lobby guards. 'I could bring him a gift.'

Willard laughed. 'You think you're going to sneak a gift past his security?'

'No,' I said – the possibilities churning over in my head. 'That's the point.'

'I don't understand.'

I kept my eyes on the guards, then glanced at my watch. A little under three hours before I had to be at the restaurant.

Yeah. I needed to find Lenny the perfect gift.

The small, silver striped box was cube-shaped. Six inches down each side, it had a removable lid secured by a blue silk ribbon. A pristine little gift-box, empty at the moment, but not for much longer. I eyed the striped lid and imagined it opening – the suddenness and the confusion. As I lost myself for a moment in the unnerving vision, Zack scurried past me down the bar. I pushed the box deeper into my bag and slid it beneath the counter.

'All good?' he said.

I nodded and grabbed a fresh drinks order.

Lunchtime, and the restaurant was busy. Young professionals mostly. Their conversations light, their laughter flowing easily. I listened to them and tried to keep my confidence buoyant – my hands steady. But my date with Lenny was just a few short hours away now. One of us was going to end up on a mortuary slab this evening, and it was almost as if I could feel the chill of the slab against my back already.

Zack headed for the fridge and grabbed a bottle of Pinot. As he did, he slowed for a moment and steadied himself with one hand – beads of sweat on his forehead. I eyed him carefully. I'd added a few drops of Dioxatrene to his coffee about half an hour ago, and it looked like it was starting to hit him. I didn't feel particularly proud of myself, but I had a bigger picture to worry about – in a dog-eat-dog world, this was a side salad.

He uncorked the wine, then paused again, blinking heavily.

'Are you OK?' I asked him.

'I just feel a little dizzy.'

'Why don't you take a break?'

'I'll be OK.'

He grabbed a handful of wine glasses, then stopped dead, staring into the distance like he'd heard an alarm. He set down the glasses, then scurried downstairs toward the bathrooms.

I nodded to myself – game time. I mixed a round of Bloody Marys, then glanced at a middle-aged couple at the bar who were waiting for a table. Mid-fifties. Wedding rings. A genteel air about them as they chatted to each other. They could be useful.

As I handed the drinks to the waiter, Zack reappeared from the stairwell – his sweating complexion pale as a pearl. I kept my eyes on him as he headed into the kitchen. I couldn't see much through the tiny window in the door, but the quiet bustle that continually emanated from beyond it seemed to dull a little. Whispers and murmurs. As I tried to make out any scraps of conversation, the kitchen door swung back open and Alice made her way toward the bar.

I drifted over to the married couple. 'Your table won't be long,' I said.

The husband nodded. 'Thank you.'

Alice stepped behind the bar, waiting to get my attention, but I kept my eyes on the couple.

I nodded toward their wedding rings. 'How long have you guys been married?'

'Twenty-two years next June,' replied the husband.

'Wow. Twenty-two years, that's something.'

The wife smiled, then glanced around at the restaurant's youthful clientele. 'We're feeling a little old here, I can tell you.'

'It's fine,' I replied, and I steered the conversation. 'It's nice serving people who don't immediately photograph everything and post it on Instagram.'

The wife laughed to herself. 'My daughter does it all the time. No idea why. I never get any photos of her, just salads and desserts.'

I shrugged. 'The mark of intelligent life is its need to share as much unintelligent information about itself as possible.'

The husband smiled. 'True.'

'Anyhow, not too long now,' I said. 'Can I get you anything?'

'Another gin and tonic, please,' she said.

'Coming right up.'

I grabbed a bottle of Bombay Sapphire and started mixing the drink. As I did, Alice stared thoughtfully at me.

I glanced at her. 'Everything OK?'

She kept her eyes on me for a moment.

'Zack isn't feeling well,' she said. 'He's gone home.'

'You're kidding, really?'

'Will you be OK covering the bar? I'll pay you flat rate.'

'Don't worry about it.'

She kept her eyes on me for a moment longer, a curious hint in her eyes. As she headed back into the kitchen, I nodded to myself. The seed well-planted.

By 3:30 the lunch crowd had gone. Quiet now, just African lounge music streaming gently from the speakers. I heard Alice emerge from the kitchen door, then started cleaning the coffee machine, trying to keep myself busy. She strolled over to the laptop by the bar and switched off the music. Four hours working to a constant soundtrack, and there was that weird silence for a moment like you were lost in space.

She stretched her back, then sat at the bar. 'Tonic and lime, please.'

'Ice?' I said.

She nodded.

I mixed the drink and placed it in front of her. She took a deep mouthful, then held the icy glass against her cheek.

'How's Zack?' I asked.

'He's got a fever.'

'Yeah, there's something going around, I think.'

She stretched her back again, then unbuttoned her smock and slipped it off. Her breasts hanging loose against the folds of her vest. Her heavily tattooed arms glistening with sweat. I eyed the tattoos – black vines and flowers sweeping in delicate strands from her shoulders to her wrists.

She ran her fingertips up and down the glass, then smiled.

'You're good with the customers,' she said.

I shrugged. 'It keeps it easy.'

She took another sip of the tonic. 'It's interesting… what you said.'

I glanced at her like I had no idea what she was talking about.

'The mark of intelligent life,' she said.

'Oh… yeah. Yeah, I was just chatting.'

'It's funny.'

'Yeah. Although, to be honest, it's not mine. It's by this writer I like.'

'I know. Zoy Rigby.'

I stared at her.

'You're kidding?' I said. 'I've never met anyone who's even heard of her.'

'I've read everything she's done.'

'Me too.'

What I'd actually read were four synopses on Wikipedia and a bunch of quotes. Her stories were depressing as hell, if you asked me, but that was hardly the point.

'She's amazing,' I said.

A hint of wonder in her eyes as she stared at me. 'What's your favorite?'

'All Roads Lead Here.'

She laughed gently to herself. 'I'm surprised. Guys tend not to read her.'

'She's missing a few car chases, I'll give you that. But… abandonment, loneliness. She knows what she's writing.'

She stared carefully at me. 'Things you know about?'

'I'm thirty years old and still working in bars. What do you think?'

She nodded.

She took another sip of tonic. 'So how long are you going to be in Miami?'

'I don't know, I'll see how it goes. I want to get to Europe if I can… work my way across there for a while. I really want to get to India though.'

'India?'

'I've never been. Plus there's a total eclipse there next year, I'd like to see it.'

'All the way to India for three minutes?'

I laughed. 'Well, if you say it like that.' I grabbed a cloth and started wiping the bar clean. 'It appeals to me, though. I'm a bit of an amateur astronomer.'

She smiled. 'You should meet my son, he's crazy about it.'

I raised a curious eyebrow. 'You have a son?'

'Martin. He's nine.'

Right. He was the stargazer – and probably the recipient of all the Star Wars gifts Alice had ordered.

'I think I was about nine when I got into it too,' I said. 'Saw my first Star Wars movie and bang, that's where I wanted to be.'

She laughed. 'Same with Martin.'

I smiled – an expression that was growing increasingly hard for me to carry. I may have been making headway with her, maneuvering myself into a trajectory that would take me into Lenny's apartment, but I could feel that mortuary slab growing colder every minute.

Alice's eyes stayed fixed on me as I continued wiping the bar.

'I called them,' she said. 'The White Room.'

I held her look. Willard had arranged a backstory for me. We hadn't had days to sort out every detail, but I'd wing it if I had to. But to be honest, if I fell at this hurdle, I think I'd be relieved.

'I spoke to Robert?' she said.

Robert Kline. I knew the name, he was the manager. 'How is he?'

'He says you're a fine bartender.'

She leaned her head back and ran her fingers through her hair. 'Why did you leave?'

'I wasn't looking for a career there, just some quick cash.'

'Then I don't understand. You could work anywhere. Why here, for nothing?'

'I like the vibe. I needed a change.' I took a deep breath, then pushed her a little. 'Look, if this isn't

67

working for you, just say. It's not a problem.'

'It's not that,' she said.

She stared carefully at me. 'I'm catering a private party tonight. I need a good bartender. Zack isn't going to be well enough. I need someone I can trust.'

I stayed silent.

She kept her eyes on me. 'Do you know who Lenny Tripps is?'

I shrugged. 'The name rings a bell, but…'

'He runs the largest crime syndicate in Miami. It's his birthday.'

'You're catering?'

She nodded. 'It pays well. I'll understand if you don't want to do it though. I asked Morgan, he covers for Zack sometimes. But he won't do it.'

'Why, it's just a party? They're not going to dump our bodies in the Keys afterwards, are they?'

She smiled and shook her head. 'It's something else.'

She paused uneasily for a moment. 'You hear about the Oregon bombing?'

'What, the… the cabin?'

'Lenny Tripps is the main suspect. Morgan won't work for a guy who could do something like that.'

'And you could?'

'I don't think he did it.'

'You know him that well?'

'I've gotten to know him. I've catered for him before. He'd never do something like that.'

I eyed her carefully. She may not have thought he was responsible, but what the hell did she know. She

68

thought I was a bartender. And as I wiped the counter clean, I could feel the anger rising in me again. The deaths of all those people. Those children.

'I'll do it,' I said.

'Are you sure?'

'It's fine. I'll serve him drinks, I'm not going to judge the guy.'

'He's a very careful man. You'll be thoroughly searched on your way in.'

'I've got nothing to hide.'

She looked me up and down. 'You got a black suit and shirt?

'Uh-huh.'

'Then go home and change,' she said. 'I'll see you back here at 6:30.'

She paused a moment. 'I can rely on you to be professional?'

I nodded. 'I'll do the job that's required.'

My heart was pounding like a jackhammer as Alice steered the car toward Sunset Marina. 7:00 p.m. and the sky was darkening above the tower. The yacht masts rocking gently in water. Alice spoke again about my duties that night, but I was on conversational autopilot – my eyes fixed on Lenny's penthouse, its lights glistening against the sky.

As we pulled into the Marina Road I eyed the guards through the lobby windows, all of them watching the car as Alice made her way down toward the entrance. She pulled to a stop by the main doors. I calmed my breathing and tried to stay relaxed. As one of the guards emerged from the entrance, I glanced at my black suit jacket lying on the rear seat. Concealed beneath it was the tiny gift-box, Lenny's birthday present now waiting inside. I listened carefully, but the gift remained silent in the darkness of the box.

The guard appeared beside the car. Muscular, but kind of awkward-looking. Thick-rimmed glasses and badly cut hair, he looked like a chess geek who won tournaments by strangling everyone.

Alice smiled easily at him as she buzzed down the window.

'Good evening, ma'am,' he said.

'Good evening, Cole,' she replied.

He glanced at me. 'He's the replacement for this evening?'

She nodded. 'Rick Sullivan.'

He leaned down by the passenger window, eyed me for a moment, then stared around the interior of the car. My nerves rattled as he glanced at my jacket lying on the rear seat. I'd managed to fold my jacket around the box so it didn't show, but that wouldn't guarantee anything.

'We can pop the trunk if you like,' I said. 'The gear's in the back.'

Alice glanced at me. 'Just let him do his job.'

I nodded.

Cole eyed me carefully. 'You have any weapons, phones, or cameras with you, sir?'

'Just a phone.'

He reached out a hand. 'Can I have it, please? You'll get it back when you leave.'

I reached into my pocket and handed him my phone. He kept his eyes on me for a moment longer, then stepped away from the passenger door.

'Report to Diaz and Hoate,' he said.

I glanced at Alice, who nodded for me to get the bags. I got out of the car, headed round to the rear and pulled two heavy nylon bags out of the trunk – all the provisions she was going to need for the evening. I laid them on the ground, then grabbed a gray sweatshirt from the rear seats. As I slipped it on over my black evening shirt, Alice glanced curiously at me. It may have been early evening but it was still boiling.

'I don't want to get the shirt dirty while we're setting up,' I said.

She kept her eyes on me for a moment, then nodded and made her way into the lobby. I took my folded suit jacket from the rear seat, carefully rested it between the handles of one of the bags and then picked them both up.

I followed Alice inside, Cole right on my tail. Two of the lobby guards ushered us into the room by the reception desk that I'd seen Alice led into before. A world away from the sphinxes and lurid gold leaf of the lobby, the room looked like a police interrogation cell. Stark and windowless. I glanced around the room – no chairs, just a long metal table in the center with a whole bunch of high-tech-looking scanners resting on it.

As one of the guards picked up a scanner the size of a baseball bat, the second grabbed a device that looked like a radar-gun.

Cole entered the room and closed the door. 'Place the bags on the table, please,' he said.

I heaved the bags onto the table, then casually removed my folded suit jacket from its nest between the handles. I placed it on the table beside the bags, hoping they'd deal with it last.

The guard with the baseball-bat scanner stepped toward me. 'Raise your arms, please.'

I did what I was told. As the guy ran the scanner across my body, Cole walked into view and eyed me – quietly, but intently. It felt like I was having an MRI scan of my personality, like any moment he was about to tell me everything that was wrong with me. I glanced at his tailored black silk jacket, a subtle fold in the material just beneath his right arm. He was carrying a holstered pistol. All the guards were, but Cole was left-handed.

'Where are you from?' he asked me.

'San Francisco.'

'What did you do there?'

'Bartender.'

'Which bar?

'The Mandarin Oriental, The Limehouse…'

'What does the Limehouse look like?'

'Like an old British pub. But big.'

I'd seen this routine before at airports. Security guards asking rapid chains of questions to rattle you, see if you begin to sweat. And I was – my hands, glistening. As the guy with the baseball-bat scanner hovered it slowly down my legs toward my shoes, the second guard with the radar-gun device started unzipping the nylon bags.

'You have family in the city?' Cole asked me.

'Uh-huh.'

'Who?'

'My mom, Helen. My dad, Richard.'

As the guard ran the radar-gun through the bags, his arm brushed against my folded suit jacket. The gift-box hidden beneath it hit the light. He stared curiously at it for second.

'Cole?' he said.

Cole stared at the box, then picked it up.

'What's this?' he said. He turned to Alice. 'We said no deviation from the routine.'

Alice looked as concerned by the find as Cole did. I hadn't told her about it – I didn't want to run the risk of her demanding that I leave it behind.

'What?' I said. 'It's just a gift. It's his birthday, right?'

Alice stared at me like I was an idiot. 'You bought him a gift?'

'Yeah, it just seemed, I don't know, rude not to.'

'What's in it?' said Cole.

'It's just a bird… a red canary. It's beautiful.'

Alice shook her head in disbelief.

Cole opened the room door and beckoned two more of the lobby guards inside. 'He bought him a fucking gift.'

The additional guards stood beside me, their eyes fixed on me as Cole handed me the box. He produced a pistol from his shoulder holster and held it at his side.

'Open it,' he said.

I stared at the box – tiny pin holes along one side so the canary could breathe.

I glanced at the ribbon. 'You got a knife?'

Cole eyed me carefully, then nodded toward one of the other guards – a stocky, bullet-headed guy in his late twenties. I'd seen him before. He was right-handed. He produced a flick-knife from his pocket and snapped it open. Keeping his eyes on me, he slowly ran the blade across the ribbon. The second the blue silk fell away from the box I lifted the lid. The red canary instantly took flight.

'Fuck!' I said.

I bumped into the guard as I reached for the escaping bird. A second of confusion – a flurry of red feathers – I slipped two fingers inside the guard's left-hand jacket panel and switched his pistol into the inside pocket of my sweatshirt. The canary flew up to the ceiling, flapping nervously as it tried to find a way out, tumbling against the light panels. Cole sighed as it started to shit across the floor.

The guy with the scanner laughed. He glanced at Cole, then placed the scanner back on the table. 'He's clean,' he said.

Cole shot me a look, then glanced irritably up at the bird.

I shrugged. 'It was just a thought, that's all.'

'We'll get it down,' he said. 'You can take it with you when you leave.'

'It's fine, just let it go,' I said.

He gestured that they should move onto Alice.

74

Alice raised her arms, then turned to me. 'You should have told me about this.'

'I'm sorry, I was going to mention it, but…'

As the canary flapped against the ceiling lights, I kept my eyes on the bullet-headed guard. If he realized that his gun was gone now, I was fucked. But he and Cole seemed too irritated, too concerned by what might be in the bags. They rifled through the contents – not that there was anything to find except cuts of fish, lamb, and a whole delicatessen's worth of truffles and cheeses. I stood still, my arms at my sides, but could feel the weight of the pistol sagging the fabric of my sweatshirt. I slowly folded my arms across my chest.

Cole shook his head as he took out the final jars and pans from the bags.

He sighed, then nodded to the bullet-head. 'Alright, take them up.'

My face sweating, I repacked the bags – Cole's eyes on me as the bird continued to bounce and flap against the fluorescent ceiling lights. I zipped the bags closed, then followed Alice out into the lobby, hugging one of the bags against my chest to hide the weight of the pistol. The bullet-head handed us over to another couple of lobby guards who proceeded to escort us into one of the elevators.

As we rose through the tower, I could feel Alice staring at me like I'd already screwed up. Not that I gave a shit. All I could think about was Lenny, taking the shot, and getting out. The elevator slowed as the floor indicator signaled the penthouse. As the doors slid open, I took a deep, calming breath and eyed the marble landing ahead of me. At the far end, a gold apartment door sat in an ornate latticework frame – three more guards standing beside it. I kept the bag tight against my chest as I followed Alice toward the door, the guards nodding politely to her as they ushered us into the apartment.

We stepped into a huge, flamboyantly-decorated reception room. It was like the Sistine Chapel inside. Cream marble pillars, everything gilt edged. The ceilings painted with blue, Michelangelo-styled skies. But no angels in these skies. Instead, galloping across the firmament were flying horses and winged sports cars. I'm not kidding – in the center of the ceiling was a bright red Ferrari Testarossa with gossamer wings flapping from its roof. Jesus. If the lobby was high on the glitz chart, then Lenny's apartment had pole-vaulted itself off the fucking map. I'm not one who cares a great deal about interior design, believe me, but it was getting easier to justify killing him every second.

'The kitchen's this way,' said Alice.

I followed her as she strolled across the reception room. Through a set of open double doors I could see the dining room – a palatial table running down the center that was already set for the thirty-two guests. Alice stopped at another gold door beside the balcony windows, the soaring masts of three yachts rocking gently below us in the Marina. She knocked at the door.

'Yeah!' came a baritone voice from the other side.

I recognized the voice from the interviews I'd seen. Its earthy tone. Alice opened the door, and there he was – the most elusive figure on the eastern seaboard. Lenny Tripps. His doughy bulk was crammed into a black suit and crisp white shirt. Dense, wavy black hair brushed back and hanging down to his shoulders. His hairy, thick-fingered hands picking at a plate of snacks as he stood by the kitchen sink.

He put down the snacks. 'Alice!'

He wiped his fingers on a towel, then swayed over to her and gave her a hug.

'Happy birthday,' she said. She glanced at the snacks by the sink. 'You're eating?'

'I know. I couldn't wait.'

She rolled her eyes.

He glanced at me. 'This the guy?'

Alice nodded. 'This is Rick.'

'Birdman!' he said.

I nodded. 'Yeah. Sorry about that, Mr Tripps.'

'Ha! Mr Tripps! The name is High-Lord-Emperor-of-Fucking-Infinity. Or Lenny. Take your pick.'

'Alright. Lenny.'

'Good choice.'

As he winked at me, the kitchen door swung open, and a woman in her late thirties wearing a white bath robe drifted in. Six foot and stunning with it, I guessed she was Lenny's girlfriend. All cheekbones and legs, she was no glitzy gangster's moll – she swanned through the kitchen like an aerodynamic poem. She smiled and kissed Alice on the cheek.

'How are you?' asked the woman.

Alice nodded. 'Looking forward to tonight.'

The woman raised a weary half-smile. 'Of course.'

Alice gestured toward me. 'This is Rick, he's going to be our bartender. This is Zara.'

As I nodded politely at Zara, Lenny stared at his reflection in the mirrored kitchen counter and straightened his tie.

'You get the fish?' he asked.

'Dover sole and truffles,' said Alice. She nodded at me. 'If you could leave the bags by the counter.'

I placed the bags where I was told. As I did, I glanced back at Alice. She and Zara chatting – Lenny still occupied with his appearance. I leaned over the bags and slipped the black pistol from my sweatshirt into the inside pocket of my folded suit jacket. I removed the sweatshirt and carefully pulled on the jacket. As I straightened out the folds in the material, I moved the pistol again and secured it in the back of my belt. I brushed myself down a final time, then turned to find Lenny standing right in front of me.

I stared uneasily at him.

'You know who I am?' he asked.

I nodded. 'I've been told a little.'

'Good, a little is good. But this is a party, and I want you to relax. You can spill stuff, fuck-up the carpet, I don't give a shit, alright?'

Zara threw him a weary look. 'Must you swear continually?' She shook her head to herself. 'I'm going to get dressed.'

'What dressed?' he said. 'It's my birthday, put on a bikini!'

As she headed out, Lenny put an arm around my shoulder. 'Alright, let me show you your spot for the night.'

He led me back into the reception room, toward a gold-plated bar area at the end of the room. Close to a hundred bottles of champagne and assorted liquors on the mirrored shelves behind it.

'This is your castle for the night, OK?' he said.

I nodded.

'I'll start with a gin sling,' he said. 'A little one, just to get the engine started.'

'Coming right up.'

I glanced nervously around the reception, then started mixing the drink. I tried to think straight. Alice busy in the kitchen – Zara getting dressed. There didn't seem to be anybody else in the apartment. Now might be the best time. The bar was nearly ten feet long – I could easily hide his body behind it. There'd be blood, but there were enough rugs and carpets lying around the room to cover it up, at least for a moment. All I'd need was a couple of minutes to get out onto Palm Boulevard.

My heart jumped a gear. Fuck it, there was no point in waiting. I eyed one of the embroidered pillows on the sofa – it looked heavy enough to deaden the noise. It would sound like a champagne cork. I ran my sweating hands against my jacket, then nodded toward the balcony windows that overlooked the darkening ocean.

'That's a great view,' I said.

'I love it,' said Lenny. 'Nothing but sea.'

He slid open the balcony doors and took a deep breath. I stepped toward the sofa, grabbed a pillow, then reached for the pistol.

He glanced down at the marina. 'Here, come take a look at this.'

I pushed the barrel deep into the pillow and raised the gun. As he spoke about some yacht down in the marina, I steadied my hand and aimed at the back of his head – my blood racing as I steeled myself. I blinked the sweat from my eyes, my finger quivering against the trigger. Come on, just do it. I squeezed the cold metal, then froze. Footsteps approaching the reception room. Fuck. I tossed the cushion back onto the sofa. As Lenny turned, I stuck the pistol back in my belt.

Zara glided into the room wearing a figure-hugging red dress.

'Could you zip me up, please?' she said to Lenny.

As he ambled over, I took a deep breath and tried to calm my maniacal heart rate.

Lenny zipped the dress, then gave her a kiss on the neck. 'You look beautiful.'

'Thank you,' she said, and she drifted back toward the bedroom.

Lenny turned to me. 'Yeah, come take a look at this.'

He headed for the balcony again, his back toward me. As I glanced again at the pillow, I heard voices approaching the main apartment door.

The door opened, the guards ushering in a flashy-suited guy in his sixties.

'Lenny!' shouted the guy.

Lenny grinned. 'Paddy!'

'Happy Birthday!'

Paddy gave him a huge hug. My heart sank. I'd lost the moment.

'Where's Lorna?' Lenny asked.

'Ah, she's still being searched,' said Paddy. 'Fucking jewelry setting everything off.' He grabbed Lenny's cheeks in the palm of his hands and gave him a slap. 'So how are you, big boy! Fifty-two!'

'Yeah, don't remind me.'

'Ah, it's just a number.'

'Yeah, and death is just a word. Come on, let's get you a drink.'

Lenny and Paddy approached the bar. I smiled politely.

About thirty guests arrived over the next hour or so. Mostly Lenny's high-ranking men by the sound of it, with their wives and girlfriends. They were a rough-looking bunch. The younger guys were in their forties and looked like your standard rhino-skinned psycho in a suit. But then you had the older guys like Paddy, who looked like they'd died a couple of months ago, but had made the effort to turn up anyhow. As for the women – Zara aside – they were pretty much all high-end Barbies. Bleached hair, seven-inch heels, and a sexy walk that looked more like they were trying to scratch one butt cheek with the other.

I kept my eyes low as I circled the table, refilling their champagne glasses. My role had shifted to that of waiter for the past hour. Dinner had been served, and as Lenny downed another huge mouthful of Dover sole I eyed him carefully. I figured that hitting him while he went to the bathroom was probably my best bet. But even though he was drinking like a fish, he was the size of a whale and seemed to have the bladder to match. He hadn't left the room once.

As I topped up his glass, he continued regaling the table with a story.

'So the Remmy boys are holding him, right,' he said. 'They're asking for three million or they're going to kill him. And I want to know that Sid's OK, but they're not going to risk putting him on the phone. So they say, ask us a question that only Sid would know the answer to. And, you know, Sid and I grew up together, so I say, when I was seven years old he broke my favorite toy, what was it? There's a pause for a minute, then this asshole comes back on the line and goes, he says it was a blue plastic helicopter and that he can't fucking believe you're still bringing this up.'

The table roared. 'Fucking Sid, man!'

'Yeah!' said Lenny.

More laughter. More glasses raised.

As I opened a fresh bottle of champagne, Paddy turned to Lenny.

'So where is he?' he asked. 'Is he coming?'

Lenny's mood soured. He shook his head. 'He's in Oregon.'

Oregon. The cabin bombing. My ears perked up.

'How's it going?' Paddy asked.

Lenny quietened him. 'We'll talk about it later.'

I went to refill Zara's glass, but she placed a hand over it.

'You need to be careful with this,' she said to Lenny.

He eyed her intently. 'I'm going to find the bastard who did it, believe me.'

I gazed at him for a moment, my thoughts knocked off balance. I shook my head to myself. Bullshit – he'd be pleading innocence to the bombing no matter what, even to his nearest and dearest. Three dead children, for Christ's sake. My job was to kill him. I took a deep breath and tried to stay focused.

Lenny clapped his meaty hands together, then addressed the table. 'Let's hear it for the chef, huh?' he said. 'Alice, get out here! Alice!'

She emerged from the kitchen, the table erupting with applause as she did. She smiled easily as Lenny beckoned her over.

'This woman,' he said. 'I swear, greatest chef in the world!'

He put his arm around her waist as she stood beside him. 'You want another restaurant? You want a chain? Just tell me.'

She smiled again, then gestured for me to hand her a glass of champagne. I poured a fresh glass and gave it to her.

She eyed the guests dubiously, a wry smile on her face as she raised her glass. 'To Lenny,' she said. 'May the eagle of good fortune circle your home, and may the hamster of Colombian trade deals nestle on your porch.'

The table cheered and laughed.

'To another fifty-two years,' she said.

The table raised their glasses. As they drank, Alice leaned down, whispered something into Lenny's ear, then kissed him on the cheek. I glanced at Zara, who looked more than a little uncomfortable with the exchange.

Alice straightened herself up and addressed the table. 'I hope you have a great night, all of you.'

Lenny threw her a look. 'What, you're not going?'

'I have to.'

'No...'

'I have to.'

Shit. I stepped forward. 'I don't mind staying. Tidy up.'

Alice glanced at me.

'Fuck tidy up!' said Lenny. 'We need drinks. Birdman's staying!'

Alice kept her eyes on me. 'Are you sure?'

I nodded.

'Good man!' said Lenny.

He smiled to himself, then beckoned me over. As I made my way toward him, he reached into his jacket and produced a thin plastic pouch full of grayish powder.

'I'm going to teach you how to make a very special Mojito,' he said.

Paddy laughed. 'Mo-ji-to!'

'It's a regular Mojito,' said Lenny. 'And a just little of this.'

Alice's eyed widened. 'Lenny...'

'It's my birthday,' he said. He handed the pouch to me. 'Just a little. Dab a cocktail stick in it.'

I nodded, then gazed curiously at the powder.

This might be easier than I thought.

Ten past one, and the apartment was quiet aside from the gentle pulse of Nina Simone. The lights low in the room now, it looked like some Vatican boudoir. Alice was long gone, as were most of the guests. Just Paddy and a couple of other guys lounging on the sofas with their girlfriends – all of them silent. All of them comatose on Lenny's special Mojitos. It hadn't smelled like heroin to me, but whatever the powder was, a single dab had booted them off the planet. I grabbed Lenny's glass and poured in every last grain of powder from the pouch – had to be a tablespoon full. I figured that would be enough to turn his brain to liquid.

I dressed the glass with a mint leaf, then waited for him to return. He'd disappeared into his bedroom twenty minutes ago, arguing with Zara. I'm not sure what the fight was about, but things had turned sour between them soon after Alice left. As I stacked away the used champagne bottles, I could hear Lenny's muffled voice booming through the apartment, Zara's accent turning decidedly French as she yelled back at him. With a slam of the bedroom door the apartment went quiet. Lenny swayed back into the reception room, dragging a hand against the wall as he tried to keep his drunken body upright. He glanced aimlessly at Paddy and the guys slouched unconscious on the sofas, then headed over and joined me at the bar.

He gazed at me, glassy-eyed.

'How are you doing?' he said.

'Good,' I replied.

I slid the drink toward him. 'Mojito. Compliments of the house.'

He stared blankly at it for a moment, then perched himself on a bar stool. He took out a cigar, bit off the tip and started to light it.

Silence as he toyed with the glass. I willed him to drink, but he just gazed miserably at it, puffing away at his cigar.

'I used to make a fine Mojito,' I said. 'But this? This wins the award.'

He stared at the glass for a moment – then pushed it away. 'Ah, not in the mood. Some birthday, huh?'

I eyed him uneasily. 'It might bring a smile to your face.'

He shook his head. 'Give me a whiskey.'

Shit. I poured the whiskey, my blood pounding as I glanced back at the embroidered cushion on the sofa beside the bar.

Lenny rolled the cigar around his lips as he gazed into the middle distance. 'I love her, you know,' he said. 'Zara.'

I nodded. 'Of course. She's lovely.'

'Yeah. Why do they want to make it so complicated then? Hmmm?'

I checked that Paddy and the others were still comatose, then took a casual step toward the end of the bar nearest the sofa.

'Wants to get married for Chrissake,' he said.

I kept him occupied, kept him talking. 'Marriage not for you, huh?'

'Fuck marriage. It's like sitting at the wheel of a self-driving car. You think you're making decisions? You ain't.'

I casually walked over to the sofa and grabbed the cushion – if he asked why, I'd say it was for his bar stool. But he didn't even notice. He just kept puffing at the cigar, gazing into nothing. I quietly removed the pistol from my belt, making sure I stayed out of the reflections behind the bar.

He took a sip of the whiskey.

'You think I'm rich?' he said. 'That I got a good life?'

I glanced a final time at Paddy and the guys, but none of them were even close to consciousness. I pushed the pistol deep into the cushion again, my heart thudding as I stepped toward Lenny.

'Bastards trying to bring me down everywhere,' he said. 'Motherfuckers.'

I carefully took aim at the back of his head.

'Fucking Oregon,' he said, his voice nothing but a whisper now. 'You hear about that? Three children. Children. Just to bring me down.'

I closed my eyes and tried to keep the steel in me alive. He was a drug trafficker, for Christ's sake – who cares if he didn't do it? He was my ticket to freedom. I squeezed my finger against the trigger, but the cold metal held firm against my skin. I just stood there, hovering.

87

A guard's voice from the main door. 'Paddy's car's here.'

The guard stared at me for a second. 'Lenny!'

The guard reached for his gun. I swung round, but the other two guards already had me in their sights. I dived behind the sofa, bullets tearing through air. As Lenny got to his feet, more guards hurtled toward the apartment. I glanced around the room. Fuck.

No other way out – no choice. I turned and sprinted for the balcony window, a hail of gunfire around me. As I ran, a bullet splintered off a marble pillar beside me – Lenny toppling to the floor as the ricochet caught him in the chest. I leaped up onto the railings and launched myself out into the night air, out into the two hundred foot drop to the yachts beneath me. The air racing past me as I hurtled toward a sliver of black between two of the yachts. Blurred masts and darkness, the marina accelerating toward me. I crashed into the water and sank deep, thudding into the mud at the bottom of the marina. I lost my breath as the pain tore through my legs – as I struggled to pull myself up to the surface shimmering only a couple of feet above me.

Gunshots hit the water as I broke the surface – I swam for the cover of the yacht decks. I'd only have a few seconds before the lobby guards would be out here. I glanced around the blackness of the marina. Lights in the distance. A beach, maybe four hundred feet away – people walking. I took a deep breath and dived back under, pulling my way through the black water toward the beach. Flashlight across the surface above me. I waited for the light to swing past me, then raised my head for a second. Another breath and I was back under, fighting to keep swimming, the pain of the impact searing through me.

I kept swimming, kept pulling at the water, but the panic in me was giving way to pain. I stopped a moment and raised my head above the surface. The beach was getting close, maybe a hundred and fifty feet. The distant hum of a power boat behind me, cars screeching out of the Marina Road. Fuck, they'd be covering the beach. I needed to move. As searchlights hit the water, I dived back down and raced as best I could for the beach.

Sand and stoned scraped against my hands as I reached the shore. I blinked the salty water from my eyes, then glanced behind me. The power boat was searching the sea maybe two hundred feet to my left. I pulled myself out of the sea and scrambled onto the beach, tourists staring at me as I hobbled toward the main drag. Cars pulling up on the Boulevard to my right, I lowered my head and tried to conceal myself in the crowds.

'There!' came a voice in the air.

Footsteps running behind me. The neon storefronts ahead of me, a blur of movement. As a camper van rolled past me down the Boulevard, I scrambled behind it, the lumbering van giving me a moment of cover as I crept into the crowds on the other side of the road. I glanced back – Lenny's men searching the crowds, two of them crossing to my side of the road. I needed to hide. I glanced at the bars and restaurants on the strip, but this was Lenny's turf. I didn't know who might be on the lookout for a guy in a soaking suit. I could almost hear his guys messaging every person they knew in the area. But The Pepper Bar – it was just around the corner. If Danny Perino hung out there, then it was a good bet the guys in there weren't friends of Lenny's.

Hushed tension in the crowds as three more cars screeched to a halt on the Boulevard.

'There!' yelled one of Lenny's guys.

I sprinted down the back streets, the pain tearing through me as I tried to get my bearings. The Pepper Bar was the next street on the right. Guys yelling behind me in the backstreet as I cleared the corner. I caught sight of the glowing pink entrance to the bar – Danny's black Lamborghini parked outside. I scrambled toward the entrance, one of the security guys blocking my path as I reached the door.

'I need to see Danny!' I said.

'Easy,' said the security guy.

'Tell him Michael's here!'

'He's busy.'

I glanced behind me – Lenny's men were hurtling out of the backstreet. As they searched the road, I barged passed the guard and tumbled down the stairs – the guard chasing after me. I darted into the crowds of the main bar, then gazed at the private room that Danny had shown me into. As I ran for it, the heavy by the door stood in my way.

'Danny!' I yelled. 'Danny!'

The guard from the entrance bounded over toward

me. 'Grab that fucker!'

As the heavy at the door took hold of me, the door opened and Danny stuck his head out. A group of five guys silhouetted against the LED screens in the room behind him.

'Michael, what are you doing here?' he said.

I caught my breath. 'I need to speak to you.'

'I can't talk right now.'

'I mean it, Danny!'

'Not now!'

I leaned in toward him and lowered my voice. 'Danny... I think I might have just killed Lenny Tripps.'

5

Danny's guys looked panicked as they bundled me through the bar toward the rear exit. But a strange kind of panic – they couldn't stop smiling.

'We'll get you out of town,' said one of them.

Two of the guys opened the rear door and checked the backstreet. Danny's Lamborghini then purred toward us. It pulled up beside the exit, its passenger door rising into the air like a railroad gate.

Danny leaned over from the driver's seat. 'Let's go.'

I dived into the car. As I swung the door closed, Danny hit the pedal.

'I can't fucking believe this!' he said. 'You're the man, Michael! You're sure he's dead?'

'I don't know. I think so.'

He pulled out of the backstreet, keeping his speed calm as he headed north toward the highway.

'What were you doing there?' he said.

There was no way I could get close to the truth. I'd play the thief card.

'I got a tip that he keeps two million in cash at his apartment,' I said. 'I got in as a delivery guy.'

'What happened?'

'They caught me. Bullets everywhere. Lenny got hit

in the chest.'

'Boom, Motherfucker!' He laughed to himself. 'Oh yeah. Don't worry, Emilio's going to be plenty thankful, believe me.'

I shot him a look. 'I just need to get out of town.'

'Yeah, yeah, we'll get you out. We see Emilio first.'

'Look, I really don't need to see the guy, I just…'

'This is a great day, fucker! You should be celebrating! You just made best buddies with the new king of Miami. Fucking shut up.'

As he pulled out onto the highway, I glanced at the passenger door, but I was in no fit state to jump or fight. Danny's phone rang. He grabbed it.

'Yeah?' he said. He listened for a moment. 'Yeah! Yeah, I know, I'm with the fucking dude, right now! Wait… you're sure?' He started punching at the roof of the car. 'Wooooo!'

He grinned at me. 'Tripps is dead, man! It's fucking real! The news is everywhere.'

I gazed at him. The pain in my body easing up as the meaning of this finally caught up to me.

I was free.

We drove south of Miami, winding down the coast until we hit Key Largo. Palm trees fighting each other for space along the sand-dusted roads. Danny slowed as we approached a solitary house overlooking the beach – a sprawling glass bungalow. All angles and reflections, it looked like a penthouse whose owner had grown weary of the lower residents and had the entire building hammered into the ground until only the top floor was visible. Given Emilio Lonos' reputation, that may not have been too far from the truth.

Danny slowed the car as we approached the stone perimeter wall of the house. Five guys with heavy machine guns standing guard by the main gate.

Danny leaned out of the car window. 'Emilio's expecting us.'

One of the guys nodded, then hit a control panel in the wall. The huge steel gate slid open.

As Danny steered the car inside, I eyed the house. Dimly lit from the inside, its sweeping windows were full of movement. Maybe twenty guys, drinking and laughing. Groups of girls huddled on the sofas – young. Some of them couldn't have been more than fourteen or fifteen years old. I'd have said they were Emilio's daughters if they hadn't been dressed in micro-bikinis. Jesus.

Danny pulled up by the door, then winked at me. 'It'll be cool, man. Emilio's cool.'

I eyed him uneasily. As we slid out of the car, Danny headed over to the guard by the main door. Danny grabbed him by the shoulders and started shaking him. 'This is the guy, man. This is the guy who killed Lenny!'

The guard stared at me a moment, then nodded. He pushed open the door, and ushered Danny and me inside. Music blaring – Latin rap – the bass hitting me in the chest like a velvet brick.

'Yo! Emilio!' said Danny.

We headed into a living room, all brushed stone and

sunken pools. The guys I'd seen from the windows went quiet as I stepped through the door. A sea of cold eyes and gold teeth.

'Danny!' came a voice from behind me.

A guy in his early thirties appeared behind us. Deep tan. Flowing white shirt. Panama hat perched on the back of his head. Kind of handsome, but with manic eyes. Every pore of his skin beaded with sweat.

He hugged Danny, then stared at me. 'This is the guy?'

Danny nodded. 'Old fiend of mine. Michael Violet. This is Emilio.'

Emilio looked me up and down.

He shook my hand. 'It's a pleasure,' he said, then turned to the room. 'Everybody! This is the man!'

The guys in the room raised their beer bottles and cheered.

'This is a great day for Miami!' he said. He put an arm around me. 'A great day for us! A fantastic night for this boy.'

As the guys laughed, Emilio beckoned me to sit on one of the sofas in the middle of his guys.

'Sit,' he said. 'Someone turn this fucking music down!'

I slouched onto the sofa beside one of Lonos' men – a bald guy in his thirties with the face of a boxer. Rubbery fat lips and a flattened nose, he looked like his face was perpetually being squashed against a sheet of glass. As the music went quiet, Emilio pulled up a chair and sat opposite me, Danny standing behind him.

Emilio rested his hands on my knees.

'You've done us a great service today,' he said. 'You're evidently a man of talent.'

'I told you,' said Danny.

'Shut up.'

Danny went quiet.

Emilio turned back to me. 'A great service, indeed.'

I nodded.

He eyed me carefully, then thought to himself a moment, clutching at the air like he was trying to catch an idea.

'But… you have to explain something to me,' he said. 'I don't understand. Why? Why did you kill him?'

'I didn't mean to,' I replied. 'It just happened that way.'

'What the fuck were you even doing there?'

'I got a tip-off that he keeps a lot of cash in his apartment.'

'Tip-off from who?'

I tried to stay calm as I spun the story. 'A friend of mine. Robbie Walker. He got it from a source he said was reliable.'

'And this… this Robbie, he's from Miami?'

'San Francisco.'

He took a deep breath, then leaned forward and looked me in the eyes.

'You see, I don't get it,' he said. 'We can't even get into Lenny's. All this risk, and for what? For cash you could have stolen more easily from a bank?'

He grabbed a pistol from his belt, and got to his feet, his finger resting on the trigger. Fuck. I eyed the door, but the boxer guy beside me placed his arm around my shoulder.

'Who are you working for?' said Emilio.

'No one,' I said.

'Don't fucking lie to me!'

I eyed him nervously. 'I'm not. Look, Danny knows me.'

My blood pounding as he pressed the barrel of the gun against my forehead.

'Why were you there?' he said.

'I… I told you… '

'Cash?' he said. 'Fuck that!'

'The money isn't the only reason I did it!'

He looked confused for a second. 'Then why?'

'Because… people said it couldn't be done. No one can get in to Lenny's. Not even you. I wanted to do it.'

He leaned in toward me, his whiskey-stained breath flowing over me like leaking paraffin.

'You got a death wish or something?' he said.

'Look, Danny knows me, OK. He can tell you. This kind of thing, I find it… appealing.'

'Appealing?'

I nodded. 'I get a buzz from it.'

He laughed.

Danny carefully stepped forward. 'He's cool, Emilio…'

Emilio glared at him. 'I'm not telling you again!'

As Danny stepped back, Emilio rested the gun against his hip.

He nodded at me. 'You know the government wanted him dead?'

'Government?' I said. 'Look, I didn't go there to kill him. I went there for me.'

I held his look as firmly as I could, but the fear in me was counting down to panic.

He slowly leaned in toward me again. 'I don't think I believe you.'

I kept my eyes fixed on his. 'Do you trust Danny? I mean, at all?'

He gazed back at Danny, sighing wearily as he mulled this over.

He eyed me intently.

'I find out you're lying…' He gestured to the boxer sitting beside me, 'Rico here's gonna cut off your arms and legs, then crush your head with a steel boot.'

I kept my eyes on him.

'You hear me?' he said.

I nodded. 'Arms, legs, steel boot. Got it.'

He carefully looked me up and down then wiped his sweating neck. 'You work for me now, you understand?'

I nodded.

'Good,' he said.

He shook his head to himself, then put away the gun.

'We got a lot to do,' he said. 'But first we celebrate.' He beckoned over one of the girls. 'Callie, make this fucker happy.'

Callie – maybe fourteen years old – walked over.

Emilio grinned at me. 'Huh?'

'Not… really my type,' I said.

'Too old?'

He laughed, then gestured to a woman in her twenties. A brunette in a translucent white wrap drifted over to me. Pretty, but stoned-looking, an empty smile on her face. I glanced at Emilio, but I wasn't going to argue – I just wanted to get out of here.

I kept my eyes out for any exits as the woman took me by the hand and led me down a narrow glass hallway. A stretch of doors at the far end. Through the glass I could see a swimming pool at the rear of the house, the beach stretching out beyond it. The woman opened a door and invited me into a small bedroom – ceiling to floor windows overlooking the pool. As she walked toward the bed, she slipped off her wrap, and smiled.

'I'm Leila,' she said.

She reached into the bedside drawer, produced a sachet full of coke, then poured a line on the table.

She glanced back at me. 'You want?'

I shook my head.

As she sniffed the coke, I stepped toward the windows and tugged at the handles. Locked. No key anywhere. I glanced back at the main door, but Emilio's guys would see me for sure if I took the corridor.

Leila dabbed the coke against her lips, then lay back on the bed like some frosted dessert.

She opened her legs. 'Come on, baby.'

I checked the floor around the drapes for the key to the windows. 'Maybe later.'

She eyed me a moment, then perched herself up onto her elbows. 'I don't do it for you?'

'No, you're pretty enough.'

'Then what? I'm clean.'

I tried the bedside drawers. 'I just need a little air. Is there a key to these windows?'

'Come here.'

She knelt up on the bed and pulled me toward her.

'I'm not in the mood,' I said.

She kissed me on the lips as she started unbuttoning my shirt.

I sighed. 'I mean it. Later.'

But she wasn't listening. My temper started to fray as she continued unbuttoning my shirt. I grabbed her hands and pulled them off me. 'Just leave me alone.'

She leaned back on the bed and eyed me coolly. 'What, I'm not good enough for you?'

I glanced at the en-suite bathroom – a tiny window by the mirror.

'I run with the crew,' she said. 'I'm not just some whore, OK?'

I rolled my eyes. 'I'm sure.'

She laughed bitterly to herself. 'Fuck you.'

As she crawled back across the bed, I strolled into the bathroom and took a closer look at the window.

She snorted another line of coke, then brushed the powder from her nose.

'You think you're special just because you hit Lenny, is that it?' she said. 'He was finished long before you showed up, baby. Me and the girls spreading the word it was him… you just cashed in the ticket, that's all.'

I eyed her a moment.

'What are you talking about?' I said.

'He was finished anyhow.'

'What do you mean, spreading the word? About what?'

'Oregon,' she said, and she laughed again. 'What, you think he did it? We were bringing him down, with or without you.'

I just gazed at her. The pool's reflection swimming around her on the bedroom wall, my mind turning over on itself. As I tried to get my head straight, I heard raised voices from out in the corridor. Footsteps racing toward the room.

Danny's voice yelling. 'Michael! Michael!'

I pulled open the door to find Danny and three other guys in the corridor.

'He's not dead,' said Danny.

I shot him a look. 'What are you talking about?'

'Lenny! He's at Rayworth Hospital. His guys have surrounded the fucking place.'

I stared down the corridor toward the living room, where Emilio was kicking the shit out of a glass coffee table. 'We finish this now!' he said. 'Get everyone together!'

'Fucking A,' said Danny.

Emilio bounded up the corridor and grabbed me with both hands. 'Your job's not done yet. You're going with them.'

I rode with Danny. A convoy of six cars ahead of us as Lonos and his guys tore back toward Miami. The glow of the city like a ghost on the horizon. Danny stayed silent at the wheel, his shoulders twitching. As he wound across the lanes, I kept my eyes on the dull sheen of a matte gray Range Rover just ahead of us, Emilio sitting in the back seat.

Motherfucker.

It was him.

All those people at the cabin. Those kids. Alice was right – of course Lenny never would have done it. Just a psycho like Emilio Lonos. Anything to bring Lenny down. Lonos could never get to him, but if he could pin something on him – the murder of Will Jerome – he could have him arrested. Turn the public and the authorities against him, have him dragged down from the tower by the police where he'd become vulnerable. I closed my eyes as the weight of it hit me.

Jesus. I'd just handed Miami to the one person who shouldn't have it.

I gazed venomously at Emilio's shadow sitting in the back of the Range Rover. As the convoy rolled across an interchange, the Range Rover veered east, two other cars following after it.

I kept my eyes on them as they disappeared into the darkness. 'Where are they going?' I said.

Danny blinked heavily. 'We're hitting the hospital. Emilio's going to clean up whoever's left at the Marina.'

He eyed me nervously as he exited the highway. 'Emilio wants you to go in first.'

I shot him a look.

'Finish it this time,' he said.

'His guys will recognize me.'

'Emilio wants you to go in first!'

He reached an arm under his seat, then pulled out an Uzi. I eyed it uneasily as he handed it to me, the gun glistening in the streetlights as they blurred passed the car.

The convoy stayed tight as we entered the north of the city. The towers of the financial district looming ahead of us – the streets around us dark and empty. As we wound our way passed the sleeping banks and office buildings, Danny slowed the car to a crawl. Ahead of us, nestled between two glistening towers, lay a dark stone shadow of a building. Rayworth Hospital. All Gothic arches and carved masonry, it looked like something from over a century ago. A fancy hotel once, maybe.

Danny pulled the car to a stop, the rest of the convoy parking out of sight in the side streets behind us. I carefully eyed the hospital. It was 3:50 a.m. and the upper floors were dark and quiet – just the blazing glow of the main entrance. Against the cold light I could see six guys standing guard. Danny eyed me nervously a moment, then wiped the sweat from his eyes. As he checked the clip on his gun, the boxer guy appeared beside me at the car door and knocked on the window. I buzzed it down, but he still looked like his face was pressed up against it.

'You're going to make this up to us,' he said.

He glanced at his watch, then nodded toward his guys waiting in the shadows, maybe a dozen of them.

'There's an entrance at the back by the parking lot… four guys on it. You got ten minutes to get in and finish this. After that we're coming in.'

I stayed silent.

'Fucking A,' said Danny.

'You're going with him,' said the boxer. 'OK, let's do this.'

Danny shot me a nervy look, then got out of the car. I stuck the Uzi in the rear of my belt, tucked my jacket over it and followed after him. As we crossed the road, I caught sight of two of Emilio's men creeping through the shadows behind us, suitcases in their hands. They headed toward one of the apartment buildings opposite the hospital – snipers, maybe. Danny and I kept low as we darted down a dimly lit backstreet towards the rear of the hospital. As we slinked passed a row of parked cars, I slowed a second. On the other side of the backstreet sat a building the size of a large townhouse. Much smaller than the hospital, but with the same Gothic style – like it might have been stables or servants quarters years ago.

'What's that?' I said.

The sweat dripping down Danny's face. 'Who gives a shit.'

'What is it?'

I stared carefully at the building. No guards. No security outside this one. A small sign behind the foliage by the main entrance.

'MRI,' I said. 'Radiology.'

'So what?' said Danny.

I eyed him carefully. 'So how are they getting patients over there? They're wheeling them across the street?'

104

Danny gazed at me for a moment.

'There's going to be some kind of a sub-basement connecting the buildings,' I said.

I eyed the reception area of the MRI building. A single receptionist at the main desk – a willowy-looking guy in his forties.

I gestured for Danny to stay back. 'Better I go in on my own.'

'Emilio said I go in with you.'

'You want Lenny dead or not? My way we get out of this alive.'

He eyed me nervously.

'It'll be fine,' I said. 'Just stay out of sight.'

I straightened out my jacket, then headed across the street toward the building. Silence in the air as I calmly stepped through the sliding glass doors.

The receptionist looked up from his phone as I approached the desk. 'Can I help you, sir?'

I grabbed the Uzi and pointed it at him. 'Put down the phone.'

He closed his eyes resignedly, like he'd been expecting something like this all night.

'Hands behind your head,' I said. 'Step away from the desk.'

He did what he was told.

'Which floor is Lenny Tripps on?'

He stared nervously at the gun barrel. 'Third floor. Palmer Ward.'

'There's a sub-basement to the main building?'

He paused a second, then nodded toward a staircase to the right of the reception desk. Beside it, a door marked 'Supply Room A/23'.

I eyed the supply room a second, then glanced back at him. 'What do doctors here wear? Lab coats, scrubs, what?'

'Regular clothes.'

I nodded toward the laminated ID tag hanging around his neck. It displayed a photo of him and his name, Matt Stokes.

'Give me your ID,' I said.

He took it off and handed it to me. I hung it around my neck, then flipped the tag so the photo didn't show.

'Open the supply room,' I said.

He edged out from behind the desk, grabbed the keys from his belt, and opened the door. I followed him inside a cluttered room full of glossy plastic cupboards and trays.

'Give me a stethoscope,' I said.

The guy opened one of the cupboards and handed me one. I hung it around my neck, then glanced down at myself. Black shirt and matching pants – standard issue for waiters and assassins. I eyed the receptionist's gray argyle sweater.

'Give me your sweater,' I said.

He took it off and handed it to me. I slipped it on – I hadn't met a gang member yet who wore argyle.

I grabbed his keys. 'You stay here. Be quiet.'

I checked my watch: six minutes until Emilio's men stormed the place. I stepped out of the supply room, locked the door, then headed down the staircase. At the bottom lay a fiercely lit concrete corridor about a hundred feet long – twenty thousand volts of fluorescent lighting humming against the ceiling. I sprinted down the corridor toward an elevator at the far end. I pressed the elevator call button, then listened carefully. The hum of the lights behind me. I secured the Uzi in the rear of my belt, tucked the sweater over it, then stepped inside the elevator.

My blood racing as the elevator quietly rose, my eyes fixed on the floor counter. Lenny would have at least a couple of guys guarding his room. If they recognized me, I doubt there'd be much time for explanations. I took a deep breath as the elevator slowed to a halt, my hand ready on the Uzi.

The doors slid open. I stayed still for a moment and just listened. The meditative beeping of heart monitors. The hushed murmur of a conversation somewhere in the distance. But no urgency to the voices, no suggestion that anyone had been alerted to my presence. A sign on the wood-paneled corridor wall ahead of me indicated that Palmer Ward was to my left. I slowly leaned out of the elevator. Dimmed lamps in the ceiling lit a corridor stretching seventy or eighty feet toward a corner at the front end of the building. I eyed the corridor for a moment, then crept out of the elevator and edged my way down toward the corner. As I neared it, I angled my approach to get a better view of the windows that stretched down the front side of the building – their reflections granting me some inkling of what might lie beyond the corner. I eyed the mixed palette of shadows and city lights, but the reflections looked still.

I calmed my breathing, then cautiously leaned a

single eye around the corner of Palmer Ward. A quiet row of mahogany doorways stretched down to another set of elevators at the far end. I crept around the corner and inched my way passed the first doorway. A patient breathing heavily in the thick darkness of the room. I eyed the name tag by the doorway: Mr. Elliot J Roaker. I nervously scanned the corridor, then went still. A man's voice from one of the rooms. Footsteps. Heading my way – shit. I reached for the Uzi, then froze as a doctor in his fifties appeared from a ward room just ahead of me.

He stared warily at me as he headed up the corridor. 'Can I help you?'

His voice loud as an alarm in the quiet of the corridor. Fuck. I eyed his ID tag – Dr Reese Burrows.

'Dr Burrows?' I said.

'Yes?'

'Matt Stokes asked me to find you. There's some issue in MRI.'

He looked confused for a second. 'Patient issue?'

I kept my voice low as I eyed the doorways further down the corridor. 'I don't know. But he asked for you specifically.'

'And you are?'

I shook his hand. 'Dr Richard Sullivan. Mr Tripps... bullet wound to the chest. They brought me over from Cedars to consult.'

He eyed my ID tag – the photograph turned against my chest.

'Can I see your ID, please?' he said.

Fuck, he wasn't going for this. I grabbed the gun,

hushing him as I pushed him up against the wall. He froze, his eyes glancing nervously back down the corridor. More footsteps emerging from one of the rooms near the far end. A man's voice. 'Dr. Burrows?'

I recognized it – Cole, the guard from the Marina. I dragged the doctor into the ward room beside me, and gestured for him to stay silent. A patient sleeping beside us, his respirator hissing in the darkness.

Cole's voice again from the corridor. 'Dr Burrows?'

A moment of silence, then two sets of footsteps began to make their way down the corridor toward the room – Cole and another of Lenny's men. I searched the ward room for a place to hide, but the footsteps were picking up pace. My heart shuddering, I glanced at the wall beside me. A fire alarm button. Fuck it – panic was going to be the best option – Emilio's men were going to attack any second anyhow. I hit the alarm – a wailing siren ringing out across the hospital. The footsteps in the corridor ground to a halt. Beyond the alarm, I could hear raised voices out on the street. The sound of running – then gunshots. As Cole and the other guard ran back down the ward, the windows along the corridor shattered, a stream of bullets tearing into the hospital.

An earthy voice from way down the corridor. 'Cole? Cole! Govey!'

Lenny's voice.

Muffled gunshots from inside the hospital. Screams. I leaned down and whispered to the doctor, 'You stay here. Stay low.'

As he gazed back at me, I crept over to the ward

room doorway and carefully leaned my head around the corner. Cole and the second guard were lying motionless on the floor – diaphanous green laser sights flickering in the air above their bodies. I stayed absolutely still. As the lasers sheered across the corridor in front of me, I tracked the beams toward a balcony in the apartment building opposite. Emilio's guys. But I didn't know whether they'd be targeting me too now.

Lenny's voice again. 'Cole? Cole!'

I ducked to the floor and crawled down the corridor, the ghostly lasers arcing above my head. I clambered passed Cole and Govey's bleeding bodies, then carefully eyed the darkened ward room beside me. Lenny was lying in bed attached to a saline drip and a heart monitor. His chest and right shoulder bandaged – his sweating bulk wrapped in a hospital gown. I scrambled inside the room and swung the heavy mahogany door closed behind me, bullets immediately splintering into the wood.

Lenny raised his head and tried to focus on me.

I eyed him breathlessly. 'We need to get out of here.'

The stupor in his eyes cleared as he stared at me.

'Mortherfucker!' he yelled. He started feebly waving his arms trying to punch me. 'Bastard piece of shit! Cole! Cole! Govey!'

'They're gone.'

'Motherfucker!'

'We need to get out of here!'

The drip stand crashed to the floor as he pulled

himself out of bed and tried to grab me.

'Listen to me,' I said.

'Piece of shit!'

'You stay here, you die, you understand?'

I produced the Uzi and held it on him.

'I'm not here to kill you!' I said. 'I need to get you out of here!'

He gazed at me a second like I was a lunatic, and I can't say I blamed him.

'Can you walk?' I said.

The venom in his eyes as he stared at me.

'Can you walk!'

He nodded.

As he dragged himself to his feet, I pulled the monitor straps from his arm, grabbed the saline bag from the stand and pushed it into his hands.

'You need to stay low,' I said.

I crept over to the door and slowly grabbed the handle. I tugged at the door, sniper fire splintering into it the moment I moved it. I grabbed Lenny and dragged him to the floor.

'Lonos' guys,' I said.

'He's here?'

I shook my head. 'He's heading for the Marina.'

The rage in his eyes as he stared at me.

'I need a phone,' he said. 'Give me a phone!'

'Just stay low.'

'I need a phone!'

I reached for the door and pulled it wide open. As bullets zipped into the room, I grabbed Lenny by the arm and dragged him across the tiles out into the corridor. The lasers searching the air above us, Lenny stared at Cole's body lying on the blood-soaked tiles. He went still for a moment, then rifled through Cole's jacket pockets and grabbed a phone.

'His car keys!' I said.

Lenny glared at me, then turned his attention to the phone. I reached into Cole's jacket myself.

Lenny swung a fist at me. 'Don't you fucking touch him!'

'We need to get out of here, do you understand!'

I grabbed the keys from Cole's jacket, then gestured toward the elevators twenty feet from us. Lenny's hands trembling as he dialed a number on the phone, I grabbed his arm and hauled him across the tiles to the elevators. As the lasers sheered through the darkness, I raised a hand, hit the elevator call button, then gazed back down the corridor. Fiery voices from the other end of the ward – a clamor of footsteps approaching the far end of the corridor. I swung the Uzi around and took aim. The elevator doors slid open – a hail of bullets thudding into the wall beside me. I fired a stream of bullets back down the corridor, dragged Lenny into the elevator, then hit the ground floor button. I ducked as the doors slid shut, bullets ringing against the metal.

Lenny's hands shook as he held Cole's phone to his ear. 'Tony, it's me!' he yelled. 'Listen! Listen to me! Lonos is on his way there. There's a file in my desk. A blue file... I need you to destroy it now! Now! A blue file. Go!'

He lowered the phone, then closed his eyes. As the

elevator slowed to a halt, I checked the clip on the gun – nearly empty. I aimed the Uzi at the door and waited for it to open.

An empty corridor appeared in front of me. A couple of bodies lying on the floor way ahead of us – Lenny's guys by the look of it. People shouting in the distance. At the far end of the corridor, a set of shattered glass doors.

I grabbed Lenny. 'The parking lot's just ahead of us.'

But he was struggling to breathe now, his face dripping with sweat. I swung one of his arms around my neck, hauled him to his feet and dragged him down the corridor. I checked every corner as we swayed unsteadily toward the rear exit. Footsteps approaching from our right – I raised the gun. A couple of female nurses ran out into the corridor. They stopped and stared at me, tears streaming. Voices approaching the rear exit ahead of us – Latino accents. Lonos' guys.

I threw the nurses a look. 'Run! Get out of here!'

They darted past us, then scurried through a door into a darkened annex. As the door swung closed behind them, I caught sight of them disappearing through a fire exit out into the night air. Lonos' guys nearly at the rear exit – I grabbed Lenny and hauled him through the door the nurses had taken. I kicked the fire exit open and dragged Lenny out into a narrow alley that ran between the main building and the towering wall that marked the perimeter. As I heaved Lenny's useless body toward the rear parking lot, he nodded toward Cole's car, a silver Mercedes 600.

Police sirens in the distance – another round of gunfire from the front of the hospital. I reached the Mercedes, opened the passenger side door, then crammed Lenny into the seat – it was like trying to push a beanbag into a mailbox.

A voice way behind me. 'There!'

Bullets thudding into the side of the Mercedes – three of Lonos' guys at the rear entrance overlooking the parking lot. I emptied the Uzi at them, then dived into the car on top of Lenny. I scrambled over his body and tumbled headfirst into the driver's seat. Lenny ducked as the rear window shattered across us. I started the car and floored the pedal, gunfire tearing into the bodywork as I swung the car out onto the street.

Lenny raised the phone and dialed again.

He waited as the line rang.

'Come on, come on,' he said.

The line picked up.

'Tony?' said Lenny. 'Did you destroy the file?'

I could just about make out a man's voice at the other end of the line.

'Still alive, huh, Lenny?' said the man.

Lenny's expression turned cold. 'Emilio?'

'How are you?'

Lenny stayed absolutely still.

Emilio laughed to himself. 'I've got a file here... I think it belongs to you. Some interesting photos you have in here.'

'Motherfucker. You touch them...'

'And what? What, Lenny?'

'They've got nothing to do with this. You don't touch them.'

'You know, I'm kind of glad you survived. I want you to see what's going to happen now. I'm going to get every hitman in the country looking for them. You hear me? Have a great fucking day.'

He hung up.

Silence as Lenny lowered the phone. His eyes dead as stone.

'You don't know what you've done,' he said.

I glanced uneasily at him, the night air thundering through the shattered windows.

6

I slowed the car to a crawl as we entered the hushed streets of a bohemian-looking suburb. Pint-sized bookshops and mosaic store fronts. White stone apartment buildings, their facades covered in exotic murals of musicians and dancers. Lenny eyed the buildings, then nodded to one with a Chinese dancer painted across the upper floors.

'There,' he said.

'What is this place?'

'Just get me inside.'

I stared cautiously at the apartment. I didn't want to risk Lenny ordering whoever lived here to shoot me, and he looked like he was in the mood to. But the building looked dark. Whoever lived here, Lenny had called them a dozen times, there'd been no answer.

I swung a right and parked the car a few streets away from the building.

'What are you doing?' said Lenny

'The car will have a tracker. We can't park it too close.'

I eyed the quiet street, got out of the car, then hauled Lenny from the passenger seat. His heavy arm across my shoulders, I dragged his sweating bulk down the sidewalk, my body aching under his weight.

116

We reached the building with the Chinese dancer. As I searched for any peering neighbors who might serve as witnesses to our arrival, Lenny nodded toward a brick pillar that supported the main entrance gate.

'On the other side,' he said. 'There's a loose brick, two or three rows from the bottom. The key.'

I propped him up against the pillar, then crouched down and ran my fingertips across the loose mortar. One of the bricks slid a fraction. I pulled it away and grabbed a dusty silver key hidden behind it.

Lenny stayed silent as I heaved him up the tight staircases to an apartment door on the second floor. I slid the key into the lock, carefully pushed it open, then led him into a small, brick-walled apartment. A lot of antique-looking furniture. Faded mandalas painted across the floorboards. As I dragged Lenny into the living room, he stared frantically at the empty bedrooms.

'Jesus, where are they?' he said.

I lowered him onto the sofa, the springs creaking under his weight.

He winced as he grabbed at his ribs. 'Painkillers. Check the bathroom, see if there's any.'

I headed into the bathroom and opened the cabinet. A bottle of Tylenol sat among a colorful assortment of cosmetics and creams. A woman's apartment – and she had a kid by the look of it. A child's toothbrush on the basin.

I handed Lenny the Tylenol. 'Whose apartment is this?'

He dialed the phone again, his hands shaking.

'Come on.'

'Who's apartment?'

'That's not your fucking business!'

He crunched down a couple of pills, then pressed the phone to his ear, waiting for the call to pick up. 'Jesus, come on!'

I headed over to the window and checked the streets. The thick shadows were starting to pale in the dawn light. Not a soul in sight. I took a deep breath and rested my aching body against the window sill.

I tried to think what my next move should be. I needed to speak to Southwest, but I didn't know what the hell I was going to tell them. Every cell in me might have been convinced that Lonos was behind the Oregon bombing, but that wouldn't mean much to Willard. He wouldn't give a shit what I thought unless I had some kind of proof to back it up.

Lenny closed his eyes as the phone rang to voicemail. He ended the call, then ran his fingers through his sweating mat of hair.

He twisted around on the sofa and stared at me. 'Who the hell are you?'

'It doesn't matter.'

'Who are you! First you shoot me…'

'I didn't shoot you.'

'Motherfucker!'

'I didn't shoot you. It was a ricochet that got you. I had you in my sights for three seconds, I couldn't do it.'

He kept his eyes on me. 'But you're a hitman?'

I said nothing.

A perturbed look on his face like he was struggling to understand anything here.

'Why do you care if I live or die?' he said.

'I don't. But I was sent to kill the guy responsible for the Oregon bombing, and that's not you.'

'That's what this is about? Oregon?' He shook his head to himself. 'Fuck, you're government, aren't you?'

I stayed quiet.

He winced as another wave of pain shuddered through him. 'So... they send you to kill me, and you decide not to?'

'If you die, the case is closed. Whoever planted the bomb gets away with it. It'll be fine for you, you'll be dead. I've got to live with it.'

He sighed to himself as he leaned back against the sofa.

'You've fucked up everything, you know that?' he said.

He stared at me, the rage rising in him again as he tried to get to his feet. 'You miserable piece of shit!'

He lunged at me again, swinging his fists around like some floundering bear.

I stepped away from him. 'You don't want to hurt me, Lenny. When my people find out you're still alive, they'll be coming for you. I'm about the only person who thinks you didn't do it.'

'I didn't do it! You think I'm so stupid I'd hit Will Jerome? I'd be the first person they looked at... fuck!'

I eyed him intently. 'It was Lonos.'

This didn't sound like it was any kind of surprise to

119

him. 'You got proof of that?'

I took a deep breath, then shook my head.

As I rubbed some life into my face, I heard footsteps on the street outside – I headed back over to the window and checked. The first of the morning's early-risers taking out the trash as they headed for their car.

Lenny shifted around on the sofa, panting heavily as he wiped his sweating forehead.

'Fuck, I'm weak,' he said. 'I need food. Go get me some food.'

I kept my eyes on the street. 'Later.'

'Go get me some food!'

He didn't look good, I'll give him that. I didn't want to have gone go to all the trouble of saving him just to have him keel over on me now. I headed into the kitchen and opened the fridge. A lot of raw ingredients, but very little that was ready made. Under a cellophane wrap was a plate of dry-looking pizza slices. They didn't look particularly appetizing, but what the hell. I grabbed the plate and handed it to him.

He peeled back the cellophane, then stared distastefully at the slices.

'I can't eat this,' he said. 'It's meat.'

'Just eat it.'

'It's got meat. Go make me some eggs.'

'Just eat it!'

'I'm vegetarian! Do you understand?'

I shot him a look. 'You were eating fish at your party.'

'Fish aren't meat!'

'No, they're underwater leaves. Cows are made of grass. Sheep are made of Lego. Eat the fucking pizza!'

Footsteps outside the apartment door – a key sliding into the lock. I grabbed the gun and took aim, my heart hammering against my chest as the door swung open. My balance wavered a fraction as a woman appeared in the shadows of the hallway.

Alice.

She went still as she stared at Lenny lying on the sofa. 'Lenny?'

She gazed at his blood-soaked bandages, then ran over and hugged him. 'What happened?'

'I've been calling you!' he said. 'Where have you been? Where's Martin?'

'He's at his dad's.'

She sat down beside him and checked his bandages. 'What happened?'

'I got shot.'

'By who?'

Lenny nodded at me. 'This fucker.'

'I didn't shoot him,' I said.

Alice looked bewildered for a moment.

Lenny took her by the hand, then sighed. 'He used you to get to me, sweetie.'

Her expression turned cold as she slowly got to her feet. She started pacing toward me like a freight train getting itself going.

I lowered the pistol as I backed away from her. 'Look, I didn't shoot him, alright. This is a screwed-up situation, I get it…'

She dived at me and punched me in the face.

'Bastard!'

'Listen to me!'

She grabbed a glass Buddha from the coffee table and swung it at me, the statuette fracturing as she heaved it against my head. I toppled against the wall, Alice kicking at me.

'Bastard!' she yelled again.

'Alice!' I said. 'He's a fucking trafficker!'

'He's my dad!'

I went still for a second and just stared at her.

'Dad?' I said.

Her hands trembling as she glared at me.

Lenny shook his head. 'Sweetie.' He gestured for her to stop. 'We've got bigger problems.'

She glanced at him.

'Lonos got into the tower,' he said.

He took hold of her hands, and eyed her intently. 'He found the file. All my photos of you and Martin. Letters. Addresses. Everything. It won't take him long to find this place.'

She turned pale as she gazed at him.

'You need to grab Martin and get out of town,' he said.

'He's at Cal's.'

'Go and get him. Stay away from the airports, you understand? Dump the car the moment you leave the city.'

She nodded.

'And you?' she said.

'Is the basement here still empty? Give me the key.'

She reached into a drawer and produced a rusty iron

key. 'But you're not…'

'Don't worry about me, just get Martin!' He froze a moment as he stared at her. 'You never gave me Cal's address, did you?'

Alice searched his eyes. 'I don't remember.'

He leaned forward on the sofa. 'Alice! Did you give me Cal's address or not?'

She tried to think, tears welling up in her eyes.

'Go!' he said. He stared at me. 'You! Go with her! You get them out of town, you understand me?'

Alice spun round, but he cut her off before she could speak.

'You can't go alone,' he said. 'Right now, this fucker's all I've got.'

I glanced at Alice.

The venom in her as she stared back at me.

We raced toward central Miami, Alice's eyes ablaze as she tore through the streets. She hit the speakerphone and dialed a number.

'Pick up, Cal,' she said. 'Please, pick up.'

A sleepy male voice answered the call. 'Hello?'

'Cal, it's me! You need to get Martin out of the apartment!'

He yawned. 'Alice?'

'Get him out of the apartment!'

'What's going on?

'Please. Just do it.'

He went quiet.

'Take him to the bus terminal on 1st, I'll meet you there. Cal?'

'Yeah. Yeah, OK, I'm leaving now.'

He paused a second. 'This isn't to do with Lenny, is it?'

'Please, just go.'

She hung up. As she wiped the tears from her eyes, I eyed her uneasily.

'I didn't know about any of this, Alice. If I had, I swear…'

But my excuses were of zero interest to her. She veered onto the turnpike and headed south. I kept my eyes on her, but trying to apologize now would be like whistling in the wind. I stared back at the road – the sunrise burning through the windshield, the heat starting to bounce off the glittering tarmac. But the cold was rising within me. There was a kid involved in this now, and I couldn't hide from my culpability in that.

The lime green bus terminal sat within a thick clutch of palm trees. The roads around it shimmering mirages in the morning heat.

8:00 a.m., and the terminal building was still quiet, maybe a dozen passengers waiting in the shade for their departures to be announced. As Alice and I stood by the ticket offices, she kept her eyes on the main entrance, feverishly scanning every figure emerging from the sun-bleached streets outside.

'They'll be here, don't worry,' I said.

She threw me a look like she wanted to stick a fork in my throat.

Her eyes then sprung wide open. 'Martin!'

She ran for the entrance, leaned down and hugged a pale-looking nine year old – his tousled blond hair framing a face that looked as gentle as it did nervous. As Alice held tightly onto him, she turned to Cal, a sporty guy in his mid-thirties. As they spoke, Cal's expression turned cold, the color draining from his weather-beaten face. Talk of Lenny, no doubt – Alice hugging Martin's head close to her chest as she quietly mouthed words to Cal. As the air between them soured, I turned my attention to the huge terminal windows overlooking the street. If Lonos was that intent on killing Alice and Martin, he'd move quickly before Lenny got a chance to hide them. I kept my eyes on the traffic rolling down 1st, the worry in me that Cal might have been followed growing with every darkened car window that passed by.

Cal closed his eyes, then leaned down and hugged Martin. He kissed him on the forehead, threw Alice a harsh look, then headed out of the terminal. Alice grabbed Martin with one hand, his backpack with the other, and approached the ticket office.

She addressed the clerk. 'Two for the 8:20 to Jacksonville, please.'

As the clerk started processing the order, Martin stared cautiously at me.

I nodded at him. 'Hey.'

Alice shot me a look. 'You don't talk to him.'

Martin kept his nervous eyes fixed on me as the clerk presented the tickets.

'That'll be forty-seven dollars thirty,' said the clerk.

Alice produced her credit card and slid it on to the

counter. As the clerk reached for the card, I placed a hand on it. I shook my head at Alice – a credit card would be too easy to trace.

She glanced at me, then delved around in her purse for cash.

Fourteen dollars and change.

'Hang on,' I said.

I checked my pockets, but my wallet was long gone – lying on the bottom of the Marina bay most probably.

Alice turned to the clerk. 'Is there an ATM nearby?'

I took her to one side. 'You can't use any cards… anywhere. You understand?'

'Then what?'

I glanced out at the street. A lot of cars, but no people. I stared uneasily at a group of passengers milling around the terminal's coffee concession. It was far from perfect, but time was running against us.

I nodded at her. 'Give me a moment.'

I grabbed the cash Alice had placed on the ticket desk, and headed over to the concession stand. Three passengers were browsing sandwiches as they bought coffee. I squeezed past them to the front of the stand.

'I'm sorry. My bus is leaving.' I handed a ten bill to the barista. 'Black coffee, please.'

As the barista turned and poured the coffee, I glanced at one of the passengers. A guy in a white denim jacket – left-hand pocket sagging under square-cornered weight of a wallet. I nudged past him as I reached for a napkin. Two fingers and the wallet was mine, flipped and secreted under the cuff of my shirt. I

126

didn't know how much cash he might be carrying – better to be safe. The second guy at the stand had his wallet in the back pocket of his jeans. The third had his in the inside pocket of his blazer. As the barista handed me the coffee, I spilled the cup a little, flinched under the heat and nudged into the two passengers. My fingers effortlessly slipped their wallets into the now bulging sleeve of my shirt.

'Sorry,' I said to them.

They'd realize any moment that their wallets were gone, but no matter – I just needed to get Alice the money, then I'd run. As I headed back to the ticket office, I slipped the wallets from my sleeve and rifled them for cash. About a hundred and twenty dollars, that would be enough for now. I tossed the wallets into the trash can beside me, then gave the cash to a bewildered-looking Alice. As I did, I slowed a second – confusion getting the better of me. Had I seen that right, or were my nerves just fried? I stepped back toward the trash can, and stared down at the wallets lying on a mound of dirty napkins and paper cups. A photograph had slipped out from one of the wallets. I reached into the trash can and picked it up.

A photograph of Alice and Martin.

My heart stopped.

Target identification.

Jesus, Cal had been followed. I stared breathlessly at the passengers by the coffee stand. As they searched for their wallets, the guy in the blazer glanced at me. In his forties. Well-built. Dark rings under his calm eyes.

I gazed at Alice.

'Run!' I yelled.

As the guy reached into his jacket, I ran for the concession and dived into him, the two of us crashing into the stand. I reached for the pistol in the guy's hand – he pulled the trigger – a bullet shattering a fluorescent light in the ceiling above us. Passengers screaming and running for the door, Alice and Martin fleeing with them. With his free hand, the guy punched at my throat. Pain erupting in me – I couldn't breathe. I freed one of my hands from the pistol and tried to hit back, but he was too intent, too machine-like. He smashed me full on the jaw, the impact dazing me. As I tried to keep hold of the gun, I freed one hand and reached for anything on the stand I could use as a weapon. My fingertips burned as they touched upon a metal coffee pot. I grabbed it and tossed the boiling black liquid into the guy's face. He buckled to the floor, a vapor trail of steaming coffee in his wake. His burning eyes were tightly closed, but his grip was still firmly fixed on the gun. I didn't rate my chances of fighting for the weapon – I turned and sprinted out of the building.

I scanned the streets for Alice and Martin, gunshots turning the window behind me to splinters. I ran toward a department store on the other side of the street, brilliant white in the sunshine – Alice and Martin disappearing into the shadows inside it. As I chased after them, Lonos' guy leaped through the broken shards of the terminal window. Another bullet zipped past me as I barged through the department store doorway.

'Alice!' I yelled.

I searched the aisles, Alice's face appearing at the far end of the store – Martin's hand held tightly in hers. She held my look for a second, then turned and ran for the rear entrance. As I sprinted after her, the guy from the terminal tore through the main doors behind me. I ducked as bullets shattered the TV screens and laptops on the display stands. Staff yelling and hiding. The rear door just ahead of me, I leaped for it and tumbled out into the streets of the neighboring block. Alice glanced back at me as she and Martin ran for the intersection. A guy in a white Audi Q5 pulling up outside a gym just ahead of me – car key squeezed in his back pocket as he got out. I slowed to a stroll, glided past him and lifted the key. No time to wait for him to disappear, I unlocked the Audi and jumped inside.

The guy stared back at me. 'What the fuck!'

As he ran for the door handle, the sound of gunfire stopped him in his tracks. He ducked down and scurried back toward the gym. As Alice and Martin darted around the corner of the intersection, the shooter sprinted after them. I floored the pedal, overtook him, then swung out onto the intersection.

I pushed the door open as I screeched to a halt beside Alice and Martin. 'Get in!'

Alice lifted Martin into the car, then clambered in herself.

'Stay low!' I said.

I hit the accelerator, the car lurching forward like it was fueled by panic. In the rearview mirror I could see

Lonos' guy rounding the corner behind us, but we were moving now. Tires smoking as I threw the car around another corner, the engine wailing as I headed toward the pink haze that enveloped the highways.

7

When I was growing up in San Rafael the town got hit by an earthquake one summer. It was nothing too dramatic. The windows rattled a little – a row of tiles streamed off the roof and crashed into the yard, but no one got hurt. But I remember the guy on the news that night saying it was a four point eight. Like it meant something. You know, if they could tell us that number before an earthquake hit, that's one thing. But afterwards? It's just marks out of ten for knocking shit over. Oh, it knocked down a school – very good, eight point three. It was the first time I suspected that the authorities, in whom I placed so much faith and confidence, really didn't know what they were talking about. Even now, I still cling to the idea that the powers that be know better – that someone out there is actually steering the ship. It's bullshit. When an agency as powerful and connected as Southwest tell me that Lenny Tripps was behind the Oregon bombing, I take it as a fact. When they inform me that he has no family, I assume it's the truth. But they don't have a clue. They're a sideshow at best. Not only was Lenny not responsible for the bombing, but his grandson was now on the run.

Well done. Nine point four.

Assholes.

I paid for the forty-eight dollars, then headed over to The Clover Inn's main building. Alice and Martin huddled in the shade of the torn canopy hanging outside the room. The motel may have been remote and quiet – just east of the Southern Everglades – but it was a nasty little dive. It looked like it had been built in the 1970s and hadn't seen a screwdriver or a lick of paint since. Wood-effect plastic peeling off the chipboard tables and chairs. The electrics buzzing like insects. A lifeless neon sign by the parking lot billed the motel as an 'authentic slice of Florida', but the place had the air of a post-apocalyptic waiting room.

I checked we hadn't been followed, led Alice and Martin inside the room, then closed the door – a lanky piece of wood that didn't look like it could stop a breeze, let alone a bullet. As Martin silently sat himself down on the bed, Alice headed over to the bathroom sink and splashed cold water across her face and neck.

I pulled back the window and eyed the Audi Q5 parked in the gravel lot outside. I needed to get rid of it.

'I'm going to head into Florida City,' I said. 'Get us a new car... some cash. We're going to need it.'

Alice paused a moment and stared at Martin.

'We call the police,' she said.

I shot her a look. 'Forget it. Lonos will have god knows how many of them on his payroll.'

'We can't just hide!'

'That's exactly what we're going to do!'

Martin stood up on the bed and tugged at the chain of the ceiling fan. As the huge, shadowy blades started spinning, I eyed Alice's cellphone lying on the bedside table. I took a long, heavy breath. Willard would be going up the walls, wondering what had happened. I couldn't leave it any longer. I didn't know what he might do if I stayed off the grid.

'I need to call my people,' I said.

Martin eyed me cautiously. 'Who are they?'

'We're… kind of like policemen.'

'Kind of?' he said.

Alice sat beside him on the bed. She put a comforting arm around him, then glanced at me. 'They're going to help us, aren't they.'

'I need to use your phone,' I said.

I grabbed it and stepped out into the parking lot – tired palms leaning over the motel like some bargain-basement oasis. I stared uneasily at the phone as I dialed Willard's number. This wasn't going to be a pleasant conversation.

'Hello?' came his voice from the other end of the line.

'It's me,' I said.

'Michael! What happened?'

'Lenny's still alive.'

'It's all over the news. What went wrong?'

'It got complicated.'

'How?'

I took a deep breath. 'He didn't do it, Willard.'

'What are you talking about?'

'Oregon. It was Emilio Lonos.'

133

'Emilio Lonos?' I could already feel the anger rising in him. 'And on whose authority are you making this judgment?'

'He didn't do it.'

'That's not your decision to make! Your job…'

'My job was to kill the guy responsible for the Oregon bombing! It wasn't Tripps!'

'What are you basing this on?'

I paused uneasily. The drug-addled ramblings of one of Emilio's girls wasn't going to help sell my case.

'Michael?'

'I don't have any proof right now. But I heard some things in Lonos' camp. It was him, believe me.'

'Believe you?'

'I'm going after him,' I said.

'Lonos isn't on our map! Killing him isn't going to mean anything!' He tried to calm himself. 'What is it you expect me to tell Southwest? That you've unilaterally changed the target? They'll kill you as well as Lenny, and you know it.'

I wiped the sweat from my face.

'I'll find proof… just give me some time, Willard.'

'Do you understand what's going on here? You're sticking your neck on the line for Lenny Tripps.'

'His daughter and grandson are in the firing line.'

This evidently caught him as much off guard as it had done me.

'Tripps doesn't have any family,' he said.

'I'm with them now. Lonos wants them dead.'

He went quiet a moment.

'Well, I'm sorry,' he said. 'That's not our business.'

I glanced through the room window – through the grimy slats of the blind at Alice lying on the bed with Martin.

'His grandson's nine years old, Willard.'

'That's not our problem.'

His heartlessness wasn't exactly hard to believe, but it was hard to listen to.

'You need to finish this,' he said. 'Just move on.'

'It wasn't him, Willard. Jesus, do you even care who did it?'

'I care who DC thinks did it.'

'DC are a long way from this. I'm in the middle of it!'

I took a deep breath. 'He's going to kill them, Willard.'

The static humming and whirring on the line as he went silent for a moment.

'Is Tripps with you?' he said.

'He's in the city somewhere, I don't know. Look, there's some really bad blood here, I'm telling you. We let Lonos run free, he's not going to stop until they're dead.'

He stayed quiet.

'I just need a little time,' I said. 'Just… keep your dogs chained for the moment.'

'Twenty-four hours,' he said. 'You find me something that I can present to DC. After that you're on your own, do you understand? I won't answer for what happens to you.'

I closed my eyes. 'Yeah.'

He hung up.

I lowered the phone, then gazed at the palm trees shivering in the breeze. Twenty-four hours. Jesus, this whole thing was a fucking mess.

I rubbed some life into my face, then stepped back into the room.

'What did they say?' said Alice.

I nodded toward Martin. Maybe we shouldn't be talking in front of him.

Alice glanced at him. 'Why don't you take a bath, clean yourself up?'

'Mom?'

'Go on.'

He reluctantly grabbed his backpack and headed into the bathroom. I waited until I heard the sound of water filling the tub, then perched myself at the end of the bed.

'My people can't help us at the moment,' I said. 'It's… complicated.'

'So what do we do?'

'I need to find something that links Lonos to the bombing… it's going to be our only way out now.'

'Can't you just kill him? You're a hitman, right?'

I dropped my head. 'Then I'm dead too. Like I said, it's complicated.'

I took a deep breath, then stared back at her. 'Where's Lenny? Have you spoken to him?'

She took the phone from me. 'He sent me a text. A doctor came for him… they're at some house in Bal Harbor.'

'I need to speak to him. At the party, he said he had people looking into the bombing. I need to know if he turned up anything.'

'He didn't find anything.'

'Are you sure?'

'You think I'm lying to you?' She headed over to the bathroom and knocked at the door. 'You OK, honey?'

'Yeah,' came Martin's voice from the other side.

She grabbed a bottle of water, cracked the cap, then took a deep mouthful. I closed my eyes a moment and tried to get my head straight. It felt like I was playing catch-up here.

'Why's Lonos coming after you?' I said. 'I mean, he wants to hurt Lenny, but this badly?'

She glanced uneasily at me.

'Lonos' father used to work for Lenny,' she said. 'Years ago. Things got messed up between them. Lenny ended up having him killed.'

My heart sank. Shit.

'Lonos never knew you existed?' I said.

She shook her head.

'Who else knows you're Lenny's daughter?'

'No one. Just Cal and Martin.'

'The guys from the restaurant?'

She shook her head. 'I didn't even know until a couple of years ago.'

I shot her a curious look.

She took a deep breath, then ran her finger through her hair. 'My mom used to date him. She was a waitress at the Copa. Back then he used to tell people he was a coffee importer. Around the time she got pregnant with me, there was a shooting at the house where they were living. She left… never came back. She used to tell me that my father was a holiday romance, that she didn't know how to find him.' She paused a moment. 'A couple of years ago she got ill… told me the truth.'

'Lenny never knew about you?'

She shook her head again.

'But he loves Martin more than anything,' she said. 'When he found out about us, he said it would be safer for us if no one knew, not even his own people. I was in Miramar at the time. I set up in Miami so we could be closer to him. And before you ask, the restaurant's got nothing to do with him. I've never taken a penny from him.'

She sighed, then gazed out at the trees like she was lost in some mistake that she'd made. 'You know, I just… I just wanted to meet him. He's my dad.'

I nodded.

I kept my eyes on her. 'I won't let anything happen to you and Martin. I promise.'

She glanced back at me, but it didn't look like she took much comfort in it. As promises went, it was window dressing and we both knew it.

Twenty-four hours to find something on Lonos. After that, my own people would be gunning for me. It was strange to think that I once considered Southwest to be my salvation. Jesus. Nine-point-eight, Michael. Well done.

But where did I even start? Truth may be the most common element in the universe, but it's the hardest to dig up. As Alice took Martin to the motel diner, I opened the browser on her phone and searched for press coverage of the bombing. Articles from the *New York Times*, *CNN* and the *Miami Herald*. I studied the reports, looking for something I might have missed – a curious quote or detail – anything that might point me in a direction.

I read and reread the reports, but nothing stood out. A couple of articles mentioned the unidentified female victim at the cabin. Apparently, the police were working with the theory that she was a call girl. It still didn't sit well with me. Jerome had been visiting friends at the cabin – the kind of friends who'd invite a neighboring family over for lunch. Was he really going to bring a call girl with him? Even if he did, where did he get her from? Did she travel all the way from Miami with him? Or did he hire her locally?

I stared thoughtfully at the phone for a moment. Local newspapers. The nationals weren't shedding any new light – maybe I was looking in the wrong place.

The nearest town to the cabin was Gainsboro. A ski resort with a population of about fifteen thousand, it sat in a valley three miles south of the cabin. I searched for local papers and turned up the *Gainsboro Chronicle*. I hit the site and clicked on the archive – a long list of back issues appearing on the screen. I clicked on the 21st April edition.

The bombing wasn't just the headline, the entire issue was devoted to it. Stories recounted by local families and businesspeople about their experiences, and how the bombing was going to change the town forever. An interview with Gainsboro Sheriff, Murray Logan. He'd been the first on the scene after the explosion. He talked about the blackened crater in the snow. The burning walls of the neighboring cabins. How identifying the victims had been a heart-breaking task. The explosion hadn't left much for the police to work with. Body fragments. DNA.

I pulled up more back issues from the months around the bombing, looking for any other accounts. As I searched the headlines, a tiny story in the June issue caught my eye. Nothing to do with the bombing, it was a follow-up story about a guy named Robert Plack who'd died in the mountains near Gainsboro two months beforehand. It seems he'd fallen to his death, not an uncommon event in mountain resorts. However, it was his job that caught my attention. He'd worked in Portland as a private investigator.

I stared carefully at the article. Gainsboro may have been a busy resort – its all-year skiing attracted a steady flow of people – but it certainly wasn't known for its violence. For a private investigator to die in Gainsboro two months before an explosion hits the town? The two events may not have been connected, but I had nothing else to go on.

I typed Robert Plack's details into Google and found Harman Plack Associates, a small three-man firm that operated out of Salem. I eyed the firm's phone number. There wasn't a chance in hell they'd tell me what cases Plack had been working on, but there might be a way around that.

I dialed the number.

A guy with a broad Canadian accent answered. 'Harman Plack.'

'Hi. Rick Williams, I'm a friend of Robert's, is he around?'

'Robert Plack?'

'Uh-huh.'

He paused for a moment.

'Were you a close friend of his?' he said.

'Used to be. We only really got back in touch at Christmas.'

'I'm sorry to have to break this to you, but Robert passed away in February.'

'Passed away? You're kidding.'

'I'm sorry.'

'Jesus, what happened?'

'He was skiing… he suffered a fall.'

'You're kidding. Shit, I'm sorry.' I went quiet a second. 'Hang on… skiing trip?'

'That's right.'

'It had nothing to do with a woman named Sally Sullivan, did it?'

'Excuse me?'

I sighed dramatically. 'Shit.'

'Sorry, who?' he said.

'When I last spoke to Robert, I asked him to tail my wife, Sally. I thought she was having an affair. I know she went on some skiing trip around then.'

'I don't think that's the reason he was there. It wasn't divorce-related.'

'She was in Gainsboro,' I said. 'He wasn't there, was he?'

They guy stuttered a moment. 'It… actually was Gainsboro, but…'

'Fuck.'

'It was a missing persons case he was working on, not a divorce.'

'You're sure about that?' I said.

'Absolutely. A missing girl.'

My eyes widened.

'Do you remember her name?' I said.

'Excuse me?'

'The name of the girl.'

I was pushing too hard now, I knew it.

'I'm sorry, who are you again?' he said.

I hung up.

The ceiling fan spun shadows around me as I gazed thoughtfully back at the article. A PI searching for a missing girl, and an unidentified female at the cabin. Even if they were the same person, what the hell did this girl have to do with Will Jerome? With the bombing? With Emilio Lonos?

As I poured down a mouthful of coffee, the phone rang. I didn't recognize the number. I stayed silent as I answered the call.

Lenny's voice at the end of the line. 'Alice!'

'It's me,' I said.

'Where is she?'

'She's safe. Martin too.'

'Let me speak to them.'

'Hang on.'

I stepped out of the room and headed for the diner. As I crossed the parking lot, I raised the phone back to my ear.

'Lenny, listen, when you were looking into Oregon, you ever hear anything about a PI named Robert Plack?'

'No,' he said. 'Why?'

'He died two months before the bombing.'

'Never heard of him.'

'What about this call girl, you know anything about her?'

'Look, just stay out of it. You've fucked things up enough as it is.'

'I'm trying to figure this out.'

He paused a second. 'I don't trust you one fucking bit.'

'I'm with your daughter and grandson, you idiot!'

'Go fuck yourself! Put Alice on the phone!'

Jesus. If he was this stupid deliberately, people would think he was a genius.

I headed into the diner – a row of cheap plastic booths and a waitress who looked like a Playboy centerfold celebrating her hundred and seventy-seventh birthday.

Alice and Martin sat huddled in a corner booth away from the milky, dust-scratched windows. I slid into the booth beside them and handed the phone to Alice. 'It's Lenny.'

She immediately slipped out of the booth and headed outside to take the call.

Quiet in the diner – just the waitress watching a game show behind the counter. Across the table from me, Martin eyed me cautiously as he bit into a ketchup-soaked hot dog.

'You OK?' I asked him.

He continued chewing, then took a mouthful of Coke.

He placed the soda back on the table. 'Mom says you shot Grandpa.'

The question caught me off guard. I glanced around the diner, but aside from the waitress the place was empty.

'I didn't shoot him,' I said.

'She says you did.'

I sighed. 'The people I work for… they wanted me to, but I didn't. They think your grandpa did something, but they're wrong.'

He glanced outside at Alice on the phone.

'He's a criminal though, isn't he?' he said.

I stayed quiet. How do you sell a drug trafficker to his nine-year-old grandson? Lenny wasn't exactly Santa Claus, unless it was a hill of cocaine his reindeer were galloping down.

Martin eyed me carefully. 'He's done bad things, hasn't he?'

'He's… he's done a few. Maybe. But, you know, you can't judge people by their mistakes. I'm sure Einstein spilled a cup of coffee, that doesn't mean he didn't know how gravity worked, right?'

Martin looked a little lost. It was a dumb analogy, but I was struggling here.

'Look, he cares about you,' I said. 'More than anything, OK? And he's… he's good to a lot of people down here. He builds schools and hospitals and stuff.

144

You know you can buy T-shirts of the guy?'

He shrugged. 'You can buy T-shirts of Darth Vader.'

'Come on, that's not fair. Your grandpa's not such a bad guy. And I'm not just saying that because he's got a lightsaber.'

I winked at him, but he remained lost in his thoughts. As he gazed out at Alice, I tried to take his mind off things.

I grabbed a french fry from his plate and took a bite. 'So you like Star Wars, huh?'

He nodded.

'What's your favorite?'

'Empire Strikes Back.'

I nodded. 'It's a good one.'

'You've seen it?'

'Of course. It's the one where Luke finds out that his father is… you know…'

I petered out – this line of conversation wasn't exactly helping.

Martin rolled his eyes. 'I don't think Grandpa's Darth Vader, OK.'

'Because… you know, there's a whole side to Vader that people don't know about. He enjoys picnics… has a range of pastel-colored summer helmets…'

He stared at me a moment, then smiled.

'You're silly,' he said.

I nodded. 'Can be.'

As he took another sup of Coke, Alice knocked at the diner window and beckoned me outside.

I glanced at Martin. 'We'll just be outside, you finish your lunch, OK?'

145

I headed out into the parking lot, the gravel crunching beneath my shoes like a cemetery path. Alice smiled through the window at Martin, then led me to one side.

She lowered her voice. 'He's arranged a plane to get us out of the country. It's landing at a farm in Eden Point at two a.m.'

She showed me the location on her phone. It was down in the Southern Glades. I didn't know the country around there at all, but it didn't look like any kind of official landing strip to me. Probably one of the midnight drop-off points that Lenny's pilots used to bring in product.

'Where's he taking you?' I said.

'East. To the Bahamas. Then a plane to Europe.'

'He's going with you?'

She nodded.

But I didn't know how I felt about that. I wanted Alice and Martin out of harm's way, no question. But when Southwest found out that Lenny had skipped the country because of me, there'd be no inquiries, excuses or explanations.

Willard would just kill me on sight.

8

My heart went out to Martin. It must have been a confusing time for him when he found out about Lenny. That instead of the woolen slippers, bowls of candy, and birthday cards full of cash that usually fill a child's vision of their grandparents, Lenny was all cocaine, helicopters, and machine guns. Lenny's cards full of cash heading to crooked cops. All Martin needed now to complete the set would be to find out that Grandma still worked the pole at Spearmint Rhino.

It was a rotten branch of the family tree that Martin had found himself sitting on, and I started to wonder what Alice had been thinking. I'm not saying she was to blame for the situation we were in, but if I had a kid, and found out that their grandfather was an infamous drug trafficker, would I have wanted the two worlds to meet? I mean, what the hell did she think was going to happen? Building a bunch of schools and hospitals might have made him a popular figure – but he was still a killer. And a brutal one.

I looked up the police reports concerning Lenny's involvement in the suspected murder of Francisco Lonos, Emilio's father. It wasn't just brutal, it was comic. It seems that Lenny and Francisco had a huge falling-out one night. No one was sure what the argument was about, but witnesses heard raised voices and the sound of breaking glass – after which, Francisco seemingly disappeared off the face of the planet. It wasn't until a week later that workers at Lenny's tuna-canning plant in Port of Savannah found the crushed remains of Francisco's wedding ring in one of the processing machines. Lenny, who claimed he knew nothing about it, immediately labeled it a tragic accident, and recalled all the factory output for that week. He then proceeded to hold a funeral for Francisco – a ceremony that consisted of burying forty-five thousand cans of tinned tuna. The pallbearers drove a fleet of black forklift trucks.

This was Alice's dad. Seriously, what the hell was she thinking?

I gritted my teeth and continued weaving through the late afternoon crowds outside Miami Speedway Track. Racing fans and engines echoing in the distance. The colossal concrete stadium like a pedestal holding the sky above it in place. I'd dumped the Audi I'd stolen that morning, and was looking for a fresh car for the journey to the airstrip. As Alice and Martin sat way out of sight by a quiet lake near the stadium, I strolled through the swarming crowds – a sea of NASCAR baseball caps and mirrored sunglasses.

Ten minutes later, I headed over to the parking lots and started hitting the thirty or so key fobs I had stuffed in my pockets. A couple of two-doors eventually responded – a Chevy and a Ford – but with the air strip out in the middle of farm land, we could use something a little heavier. I kept on with the push-button lottery. I raised a curious eyebrow as a deep red Porsche 911 lit up. Not so long ago, I'd have jumped straight into it, but it would have a tracker for sure. Plus, I was a family man now and I needed to steal accordingly. I kept on pushing. The tail lights of an old Toyota Land Cruiser lit up. I eyed it for a moment – beaten-up, but sturdy-looking. Heavy-duty tires. It wasn't pretty, but no one was going to miss it. I grabbed the best part of four hundred dollars I'd lifted, dumped the wallets and car keys in the trash, then climbed into the Toyota. I pulled out of the stadium and drove to the lake – Alice and Martin sitting quietly by the water side.

I pulled up beside them and buzzed down the window. 'Let's go,' I said.

We headed out of Florida City and drove northwest, the sky a deep orange across the mangroves in the distance. Alice and Martin stayed quiet as they sat in the back, but that was fair enough. The drive into the Everglades was likely to be the last view of American soil that either of them would have for a long time. Me too, maybe. If I stayed after this, chances are I'd end up in a riverbed somewhere with a bullet hole courtesy of Southwest. I could take the plane along with them, perhaps – but then Lonos would walk free, and all this would have been for nothing.

As the sky darkened, my thoughts returned to the PI, Robert Plack. Who he'd been searching for? What I needed was access to his firm's files – the names and cases. Hacking was well out of my league, but Southwest had people who could do it. I glanced at the phone lying on the passenger seat, then picked it up. In no mood to speak to Willard, I emailed him Plack's details along with a request for all case information from Plack's firm. I didn't hold out much hope that he'd arrange it – he'd made his mind up about Lenny already – but I was low on options.

As the email disappeared off into the ether, I pulled up the *Gainsboro Chronicle,* and handed the phone back to Alice.

'What's this?' she said.

'Go into the archive and see if you can find anything about missing girls… runaways, anything.'

'Is this to do with the bombing?

'I've got a dead private detective who was searching for a missing girl, and we have an unidentified female at the cabin… call girl, maybe. If they were the same person it would be a huge step forward.'

She pulled up the archive, then glanced at the dates. 'How far do you want me to go back?'

I shrugged. 'Just keep reading.'

As she started searching the archive, I turned off the highway toward the darkening haze of the Everglades, the car crunching along the narrow dirt tracks. A few farm houses and tin-roofed shacks visible through the trees, but not a soul in sight. Then again it was getting late. Plus this was alligator country, and it was probably a good idea not to venture too far from either a rifle or a decent set of stairs.

I navigated the winding route through the swamps and farms. Windmills and water-towers punctuating the shadowy trees on the horizon. In the rear view mirror, I could see that Martin had fallen asleep on the back seat. I switched on the radio, turned the volume right down, then tuned into the first news station I could find. WKPM Miami, news on the hour. As the stillness of the Glades drifted by, the newscaster's voice whispered about a spate of gang-related shootings. Eight dead in Allapattah. A car bomb in Little Haiti. A nightclub shooting in Coconut Grove. I listened carefully as the whispering voice counted the dead. Lonos making his move on the city.

'Turn it off,' said Alice.

I did as she asked. She rolled up a jacket, carefully placed it under Martin's head, then returned to the archive on the phone.

As she continued browsing the pages, she glanced at me in the rearview mirror.

'So have you ever actually read anything by Zoy Rigby?' she said.

I stared at her for a moment, then shook my head.

She eyed me cautiously. 'So…'

'I took your phone. That night we met at the restaurant. I'm sorry, but I needed you to take me to Lenny.'

She nodded to herself.

'So who are you?' she said. 'Is your name even Rick?'

'I'm nobody. A pickpocket.'

'But you work for the government?'

151

I nodded. 'I want out. They said if I did this job, they'd give me my freedom.'

'And take away Martin's and mine in the process.'

I stayed quiet. Saying sorry wasn't going to cut it any more.

She eyed me bitterly, then stared back at the phone. She continued swiping pages, then slowed a moment.

She sat upright. 'Samantha Lederer,' she said. 'A service was held at Grace Community Church in memory of the student who disappeared at Gainsboro Gala.'

I glanced at her in the rearview mirror. 'Gala? When?'

She scanned the rest of the article.

'Four years ago,' she said.

Four years?

I pulled the car to a halt. 'Give me the phone.'

On the screen was a photo of the girl. Fresh-faced, she couldn't have been more than eighteen or nineteen years old. Pretty. The kind of beauty that might attract the wrong kind of attention. I eyed the article carefully. But how could she be the girl at the cabin? Samantha Lederer disappeared four years ago. How could she have been missing that long only to turn up in Gainsboro a few months ago? I gazed at the article, struggling to get a handle on it. Abduction maybe? But she'd been with Will Jerome and a bunch of other people – I doubted any of them had been holding a gun to her head. Amnesia maybe, but a neighbor, or someone in town, would surely have recognized her. She might have run away deliberately, but then why return? And under what circumstances?

I shook my head to myself. The more I thought about it, the more it failed to add up. She couldn't have been the unidentified victim at the cabin.

Alice leaned forward on the back seat. 'Not her?'

I gazed at the photo. 'I don't know, I doubt it.'

'The archive doesn't go back much further.'

'I'll call the paper in the morning... see if they know of anybody else.'

She nodded.

'Even if she is the girl,' she said. 'What's this got to do with Emilio Lonos?'

Yeah. It was a good question. Lonos blows up the cabin, kills Will Jerome – pins the whole thing on Lenny. Fine. So what's this girl got to do with anything?

I sighed despondently. 'I don't know.'

Maybe I was just chasing a dead end. That whoever this missing girl was, she had nothing to do with anything.

Fuck.

As Alice checked on Martin, I put the car into gear and pulled back out onto the road – Samantha Lederer's photo smiling from the phone on the seat beside me.

It was 1:40 a.m. by the time we passed a beaten-up metal sign telling us that we were entering Eden Point. Thickets and swamps around us. Twisted roots and insects. God knows why anyone would give this place a name, let alone Eden. The headlights picked out an anonymous track through the trees. Beyond that it was sheer darkness – the view from the windows like a shroud of black felt had been thrown over the car. I cleared another ragged, overgrown corner, then slammed on the brakes. Two guys with shotguns were staring at us as they stood in the road about thirty feet ahead. Insects swimming around them in the iodide blaze of the headlights. One of the guys raised his gun and strolled over to us. In his forties. Gaunt. The few strands of hair on his head glued down with sweat to his glistening skull.

Alice wound down her window. 'Lenny's expecting us,' she said.

The guy took a quick look inside the car, then glanced at me. 'Take the road another couple of hundred feet. You'll see it.'

I gently pressed the pedal, the guys following us at a relaxed stroll as we continued through the mangroves. The track opened out onto a tiny strip of grassland cut between the trees. Maybe five hundred feet long, but narrow – barely enough space for a small plane to land without brushing its wing-tips against the creeping branches on either side. At the far end sat a small wooden barn with boarded up windows. A black Mercedes G-Class parked in front of it. As I pulled up beside the barn, one of the Mercedes' rear windows slid open. Lenny's face appeared in the dim ceiling lights of the car.

Alice nudged Martin awake. 'Sweetie, we're here.'

Martin opened his eyes and looked around. Lenny caught sight of him, then pushed open the door and limped out of the car. New clothes. Fresh bandages. His face still greasy with sweat, but he looked a lot better than he had done last night.

Martin smiled, then got out of the car. 'Grandpa.'

Lenny hugged him with one arm. 'How's my man?'

Martin nodded and held tightly to him.

'It's all good,' said Lenny. He leaned down to Martin's eye level. 'We're going on a little vacation. Your mom tell you? It's going to be great.'

Martin nodded again, but with those same careful eyes.

He stared at the bandages across Lenny's chest. 'Does it hurt?'

'Grandpa's a tough old bird,' said Lenny. He smiled wistfully at him. 'But we gotta move quickly, so you do what your mom and me tell you, OK?'

In the rear seat, Alice grabbed her bag and slid out of the car. As she did, she stopped and stared at me.

'I guess this is goodbye,' she said.

I nodded.

She hovered a moment, then sighed. 'It's a shame. At the restaurant… I liked you there for a moment.'

I held her look.

'Take care of Martin,' I said.

She kept her eyes on me for a second, then stepped out of the car and headed for Lenny.

He put an arm around her, then gestured toward Martin. 'Take him inside. There's food, water.'

She grabbed Martin by the hand and led him toward the barn. As they headed away, Martin turned and waved goodbye to me. I waved back – reassuring myself that, no matter how this panned out for me, at least he'd be safe. As I watched him disappear into the barn, the guys with the shotguns appeared way down the airstrip. The gaunt-looking one checked his watch, then strolled over to Lenny and took him to one side. He spoke briefly to him before heading into the barn himself. A couple of seconds later and two ragged ribbons of LED lights flickered into life all the way down the edges of the strip.

I stared up at the sky. Thick clouds concealing the stars. I listened carefully, but no sound in the darkness other than the cicadas chirping away around us.

Lenny limped toward me and rested himself against the car door.

'Alice told me about the bus terminal,' he said. 'I'm grateful.'

I nodded.

'At least you do a better job keeping people alive than you do killing them,' he said.

I raised a vague smile.

Leaves rustling in the breeze. A whisper of movement. I stared into the darkness of the trees, then glanced at the second guy with the shotgun, waiting down the strip. I eyed him a moment. In his thirties. Goatee. A little healthier-looking than the other guy, but still – an uneasy air about him as he kept his eyes on the sky.

'That guy always look so nervous?' I said.

Lenny shrugged. 'When the planes land, everyone is.'

I could hear it now – a distant hum way above us. I

gazed up at the murky sky and caught sight of a small two-engine plane appearing beneath the clouds. It rocked around in the wind as it banked toward the strip.

I took a deep breath – there was no use in waiting any longer. I put the car into gear.

'Good luck with Lonos,' said Lenny. 'We'll see each other again, I'm sure.'

'Why don't you just stay gone?' I said. 'Be a grandpa for once.'

He smiled.

As the plane weaved and tilted on its approach, I swung the car around and headed back through the trees. The tiredness catching up with me now. I needed to rest – time to think. The PI's missing girl looked like she was a dead end, and I had nothing else to go on. As I struggled to get my head straight, I swung around a sharp bend in the mangroves, then slowed a little. A sense of movement in the edges of my vision. I stared through the thick trees. Stillness for a moment as my eyes adjusted to the darkness – then an indistinct shadow sprinting through the branches, away from the airstrip. I pulled to a stop, grabbed a torch from the glove compartment and shone it out of the window. The figure froze in the beam – a shotgun in his hand. The guy with the goatee. I eyed him a second. What the hell was he running from? As he continued sprinting, I turned and stared back through the trees. The plane descending toward the airstrip.

My heart jumped a gear. Fuck – he was running from what? I put the car into reverse and hit the pedal hard, branches hammering against the bodywork as I wound back through the trees. I buzzed down the window and started yelling toward the air strip.

'Alice! Get out! Lenny!'

I reached the strip and veered toward the barn.

I yelled again. 'Alice!'

A bullet rang out and shattered the Toyota's rear window. I ducked down in the seat, kept my foot hard on the pedal. Another stream of bullets thudded into the bodywork, the car crunching into the side of the Mercedes. As the car shuddered to a halt, I carefully raised my head. Lenny emerging from the barn – the plane coming in to land. As Lenny stared at me, a brilliant flash erupted through the branches on the other side of the strip, then soared into the sky. A bone-jarring crack as the plane erupted into a ball of flame. It dropped from the treetops then tumbled down the strip – propellers and flaps tearing off as it careered down the grass and slammed headlong into the barn. Gunfire in the air. Figures emerging from the trees down the strip. Six or seven of them. Lonos' guys. That goatee fucker had sold us out. I jumped out of the Toyota, bullets zipping through the air around me. I arced round the flaming wreckage of the plane, covered my face with an arm, then kicked down the smoldering slats of one of the barn doors.

'Alice!' I yelled. 'Martin!'

Bullets tearing through the smoke. I ran over to Lenny and Alice – Alice trying to pick Martin up off the floor. Her face bleeding as she grabbed him and held him close to her chest. Another explosion as the heat ignited the Mercedes' fuel tank outside. Fuck, they'd be here any second. Lenny rose to his feet, the fury driving him like a machine.

'Motherfuckers!' he yelled.

He flung open a steel chest on the barn floor and grabbed a heavy-caliber automatic rifle. He gestured for me to take Alice and Martin out the rear door of the barn. As I grabbed them and ran out into the darkness, Lenny stepped toward the plane wreckage like a man possessed – spraying a stream of bullets through the flames. I picked up a smoldering splinter of wood from the ground, then led Alice and Martin through the trees. I stopped by a dense clump of twisted roots about eighty feet from the barn. I checked behind us, then signaled for Alice and Martin to hide under the roots. I nodded for them to just stay there, held tightly to the burning splinter of wood, then darted away into the darkness.

I weaved through the trees, igniting wisps of sawgrass in my wake. More gunshots from the barn way behind me. I glanced back at the faint trail I'd left in the undergrowth, then kept running – another two, three hundred feet before I stopped and tossed the burning splinter as far as I could. The crackling of the barn in the distance, black smoke creeping through the undergrowth. I darted away from my makeshift trail, then ducked low in the undergrowth.

Footsteps stumbling through the fauna way off to my right – Lenny's silhouette through the trees. As he followed the trail toward me, I reached out from the foliage and grabbed him, immediately raising my hands as he swung the rifle around. I pulled him away from the trail and led him back toward the roots where Alice and Martin lay hidden. We stopped dead as hushed voices emerged from the barn. I listened intently as they headed out into the trees, at least five of them. They'd split up – fan out – but they'd keep in the direction of the trail. As I kept my eyes on the darkness, a silhouette weaved past the embers in the sawgrass, the ugly lines of an automatic weapon pointing ahead of him. As Lenny raised his gun, I grabbed hold of him. Now wasn't the time – just let the guy follow the trail. My heart thumping against my chest as the figures started to arc away from us. I took hold of Lenny and led him back toward Alice and Martin, pushing my feet flat across the forest floor to nudge away any loose branches or twigs that might signal our location. We reached the twisted clump of roots. I crouched down to find Alice holding Martin behind her. I scanned the barn – a single armed figure waiting by the burned-out shell of the Mercedes. The Toyota in flames beside it. I gazed down the airstrip. Lonos' guys had emerged from the trees on the left-hand side. They'd have cars somewhere nearby – parked out of earshot, but within reach of the strip. I nodded at Lenny, then signaled for Alice and Martin to follow us.

We kept low within the foliage as we arced around the remains of the barn, the guy by the Mercedes disappearing from sight as we crept through the trees by the airstrip. As I led the way I searched for anything that might reflect the soaring flames behind us. A glinting windshield or glowing wheel rim. I scanned the darkness but there was nothing. Just shadows and silhouettes.

Voices way behind us. I couldn't make out what was being said, but the tone was aggressive now, like they'd found the end of the trail. They'd spread out and cover as much of the area as they could. We'd need to move quickly. As I kept Lenny on his feet, I searched the shadows through the trees. No reflections, but there was something else. I went still. A man's voice in the distance – on his own, talking on a phone. About twenty degrees to our left.

I turned back to Lenny. 'Give me the gun. Wait here.'

He eyed me for a second, then handed me the weapon.

I ducked low beneath the branches and began creeping in the direction of the voice. I kept the gun aimed ahead of me as I silently pushed my way through the trees, the air around me thick with insects. My heart pounding, I slowed to a stop. In the darkness ahead of me, I could just about make out a clearing, maybe fifty feet ahead. Two black Jeeps parked by a narrow dirt track that weaved through the mangroves on the other side. I stared intently at the cars. No voice in the air now. I crept a little further toward the cars, scanning the darkness around them.

'Don't move,' came a voice from beside me.

I froze.

'Drop the gun,' he said.

I did what I was told.

I slowly turned to find a thick-necked Hispanic guy pointing an Uzi at me. I only vaguely remembered him from my encounter with Lonos, but he definitely remembered me.

'Motherfucker,' he said.

My blood racing as he raised the gun toward my head.

'Where's Lenny?' he said.

I just stared at him.

'Where's Lenny!'

I nodded toward the darkness just behind him. 'Just there.'

For a second his eyes diverted from me – I grabbed the Uzi with one hand and jabbed my elbow deep into his throat. As I tried to pull the gun from his hand, he grabbed at me – started yelling into darkness.

'Rico!' he said. 'Here!'

We tumbled to the ground, fighting for the weapon.

'Rico!' he yelled.

He smashed me in the face. Dazed, I felt the gun slip from my hands. I looked up to see him swinging the gun toward me. He took aim, then toppled to one side as Lenny's huge bulk crashed into him out of the darkness. As the guy struggled to free himself from Lenny's gargantuan arms, I dragged the gun free from his hands and aimed it at his head. He went still, stared at us a second, then yelled out again. Lenny swung his boot down onto the guy's face. A dull crack of bone and the guy went quiet – groaning weakly as he rolled on the ground.

I turned to find Alice and Martin silhouetted against

the distant flames of the barn. As they caught up to us, I nodded toward the cars.

'Let's go,' I said.

The guy choking on the ground.

Lenny glared down at him. 'Piece of shit.'

He started kicking at the guy's head.

'Let's just get out of here,' I said.

Lenny's face nothing but shadow in the infernal glow behind him. He grabbed the gun from me, swung it around, and hammered the butt down onto the guy's skull. Again and again, until the sound went soft.

I glanced at Alice and Martin standing in the trees behind him – Martin clutching Alice's side. As Lenny continued hammering the gun down on the guy, I pulled him away.

'He's finished! Let's go.'

Lenny glared at me a moment, then stormed back toward the guy like a fucking possessed bull.

I grabbed onto him. 'You really want Martin to see this? Let's go!'

He went still, panting as he stood over the guy's motionless body. He caught his breath, then glanced at Martin cowering behind his mother.

Alice took Martin by the hand and led him toward the Jeeps. Martin quiet as the grave as he stared back at the shadow of his grandfather.

9

The rage in Lenny. It took me by surprise. He may have run the Miami drug scene, but the way he crushed that guy's skull – and in front of Martin – it chilled me. For his grandson to hear stories about him was one thing, but to see something like that? That shit stays with you. It changes you. I didn't want Martin thinking this kind of behavior was in his blood, in nature. Ending up as some disturbed teenage student who gets voted 'Most Likely to be Shot by a SWAT Team'.

The car rattled and bounced as I weaved it through the snaking tracks of the Glades. Martin little more than a shadow on the backseat as he lay with his head burrowed into his mom's lap. As we passed the quiet homesteads and shacks that marked the outer edges of the wetlands, I glanced at Lenny – beads of sweat streaming down his cheeks, his eyed fixed ahead of him. The anger in him simmering now. He wiped the sweat from his forehead, then coughed. A splatter of blood in his palm. It looked like his wound had ruptured, become infected, maybe. Either way, he looked bad. As he wiped his hand against his shirt, I eyed him carefully.

'We need to switch cars,' I said. 'Then find a place to spend the night. Somewhere you won't be recognized.'

He winced as he stared back at Alice and Martin.

'I'll find us a way out of this, don't worry,' he said.

He nodded reassuringly at her, but the desperation in him was plain to see. The tide had turned against him, and he was running out of people he could trust.

The angular wooden house stood on its own in a half acre of tired-looking elms just north of the Glades. The overgrown lawn waving in the breeze like a pool. No car in the driveway, nor the garage. I checked the ground floor windows, then quietly scaled the guttering and took a look in the bedroom windows. No signs of life anywhere. Bare mattresses. I glanced out across the trees – the nearest houses were at least two hundred feet away. I stared again through the bedroom windows, then nodded to myself. This would serve as home for the night.

I slipped back down to the ground, then headed for the car – a 2006 Chevy Silverado that I'd picked up in a gas station just outside town. As Alice and Martin helped Lenny out of the car, I headed to the trunk and took a look inside. A large steel tool box. I opened it up. Lying among the wrenches and screwdrivers was a bottle of engine oil and a couple of stained rags. They would do the trick. I grabbed the oil and one of the rags, then headed for the rear door of the house. I didn't know much about picking locks, but it was nearly three a.m. and the sound of breaking glass would carry some distance. As Alice and Martin helped Lenny toward the house, I poured the viscous oil across a glass panel beside the rear door. I laid the rag against it, then nudged at the glass with my elbow. The glass broke with a dull crunch, the pieces stuck firmly to the material. As I carefully pulled the glass away, Alice and Martin led Lenny toward the house.

Lenny tripped on an elm root as he crossed the yard. 'Bastard fucking trees,' he said.

I shot him a look. 'Quiet.'

I reached an arm inside the window and clicked open the door.

'Fucking ground,' he said.

'Will you shut up?' I said. 'I'm trying to get you guys safe.'

'Yeah, you're a real hero. What, you leave your keys in your other cape?'

Alice took him by the arm. 'Lenny, please?'

He glanced at her, then quietened himself as we led him inside the house.

Plastic sheeting thrown over the flower-patterned sofas in the living room. All the tabletops clean. The TV unplugged from the wall socket. I relaxed a little. Whoever lived here had been gone for a while by the look of it. We helped Lenny up the narrow staircase toward the first bedroom we found. The sweat glistening across his face as Alice and Martin gently lowered him onto one of the mattresses.

'Give me the phone,' he said.

I shook my head. 'No phones. We shouldn't even be carrying it.'

'How the hell am I going to get them out? I need to make some calls.'

166

He grabbed the phone from Alice.

'Just be careful,' I said.

He shot me a look. 'Really? Because I was about to ask Lonos if I could borrow his fucking speedboat!'

I sighed to myself, then glanced at Martin.

'Let's leave your grandpa to it,' I said. 'You should try and get some sleep.'

He stared at Alice.

She nodded. 'I'll be there in a moment, sweetie.'

Martin followed me out of the room. I took a quick look around one of the bedrooms further down the landing, then ushered him inside.

'It's fine,' I said. 'We'll be safe here.'

He didn't look that comforted by my assurance. His expression was like stone. I stayed in the doorway as he headed over to the bed and sat down on the mattress.

'Try to get some sleep,' I said.

I waited a moment, but he just stared into the darkness. Didn't move. Didn't make a sound. I took a deep breath, then stepped into the bedroom and sat down beside him.

'It was a bad night, I know,' I said. 'But we're here, and... it's going to be OK.'

He stayed quiet.

I stared out of the window for a moment. The trees like charcoal scratches against the moon.

'It won't always be like this,' I said. 'We're just... we're having the worst of it right now. Your grandpa's got some enemies, but he's going to keep you safe. We all are. You can be sure of that.'

He gazed down at his hands.

'He killed that man,' he said.

'Of course he did. He was trying to protect you.'

He nodded vaguely.

'He's killed a lot of people, hasn't he?' he said.

I took a deep breath. 'I don't know. But soldiers kill people too. You think they're bad?'

'He's not a soldier.'

'No, but… the people he's hurt, they're not good guys, believe me.'

'No. They're the same as him.'

I sighed. 'Martin…'

He stared carefully at me. 'Do you like him?'

I kept my eyes on him. 'I like you.'

'Listen to me,' I said. 'You're nothing like him. You never will be. I know he's your grandpa, but…'

He stayed quiet as he toyed with the straps on his backpack.

He shook his head to himself. 'He's angry all the time. Shouts at people.'

'I know.'

'He curses all the time,' he said.

'I know. But so do I.'

He glanced at me. 'You do. It's not good.'

I winked at him. 'You see, you're better than both of us already.'

A wistful smile lightened his face a little.

'Hey, you want to learn how to curse without being rude?' I said.

He eyed me curiously.

'The verb my noun rule,' I said. 'It's simple. You

take any verb you like, and noun you like... stick *my* in the middle and you're being rude. Hey, fax my chicken! Bake my biscuit!'

I nodded at him. 'Go on, give it a try.'

He thought to himself a moment. 'Dent... my bucket?'

'Dent my bucket! You see? You're being rude, but you're not.'

'What are you teaching him?' came Alice's voice from the door.

I shook my head. 'Ah, nothing.'

I smiled at him again, then got to my feet.

'Get some sleep,' I said. 'Dent my bucket... you and I are buddies for life now, you know that?'

He smiled.

I headed over to Alice. 'I'll keep watch. You get some rest too. '

She held my look for a moment, then nodded.

I headed downstairs and gazed out at the sleepy houses in the distance – my regret at Martin's involvement in all of this stinging at me. I'd have sooner run from Southwest than see Martin go through all of this. It was a desperate mess. I headed into the kitchen and perched myself by the window. The tiredness aching in me, I opened a few of the cupboards. Piles of dusty plates and cups. An old jar of instant coffee sitting at the back of the shelf, the granules clumped together inside it like chunks of Martian rock. I scraped a few rocks out of the jar, then hit the kettle.

Silence. Just the house creaking in the breeze – the

quiet, leafy roads outside. As I sipped the coffee, I glanced at a neatly stacked pile of letters on the kitchen table. I reached for them, then sat back down at the window. The letters were all addressed to Larry and Jennifer Harding. The post marks from nearly two months ago. They were on holiday probably. The pictures on the fridge showed a couple in their late sixties standing proudly beside a shiny new Winnebago. I nodded to myself – we were good for the moment. As I placed the letters back on the table, I caught sight of movement outside. I stayed still in the shadows as a guy wearing a tan shirt and matching pants emerged into the moonlight from a neighboring house just past the trees. He glanced in my direction as he sat on a porch chair and lit a cigarette – the amber glow like a warning light in the distance.

As I stayed low by the window, I heard footsteps coming down the stairs.

Alice appeared in the kitchen doorway.

'Keep the lights off,' I said. 'There's a guy outside, a neighbor.'

She edged over to the window and took a look.

'Everything OK?' I asked.

She nodded. 'They're asleep.'

She kept her eyes on the neighbor for a moment, then sat down at the kitchen table.

'Did Lenny speak to anyone?' I said.

'He might have arranged a boat. We'll know in the morning.'

'Then get some rest, you're going to need it.'

'I can't.'

She wearily ran the fingers of both hands through her hair.

'There's coffee if you want,' I said.

She shook her head, then slouched back in the chair. She took a deep breath.

'You think I made a mistake getting Martin involved with him, don't you?' she said.

I glanced at her.

'Not a mistake,' I said. 'But…'

'He needed a father figure. Cal was never that involved with him.'

'You guys are divorced?'

'We weren't married. It's pretty much always been just me and Martin.'

She went quiet as she bathed in the moonlight. Her expression distant as she gazed up at the sky.

'Martin watches the stars all night,' she said. 'Grabs his telescope, heads up onto the roof. He's there for hours. It feels like he's trying to escape from me sometimes.'

'I don't know. I used to do magic when I was his age. Lock myself away all night, practicing. It's just dreams. I wouldn't take it personally. Plus he's a great kid. You must have done something right.'

She raised a smile.

The neighbor stubbed his cigarette out against the porch rail, then flicked it out onto the road. I kept my eyes on him as he headed back inside.

Alice reached for my coffee cup and took a sip. 'So tell me, what's a pickpocket doing working for the government?'

'Same as everybody else. Sticking their hands where they're not wanted.' I paused a moment, then shrugged. 'I used to steal cars, but… it got complicated.'

'They caught you?'

'Not exactly. But I'm kind of stuck with them at the moment.'

'What would you do if they let you go?'

I stared at her. It was a question I hadn't actually given much thought to. All I knew was that after ten years of stealing sports cars, then a year killing for the government, I had no desire for any kind of excitement.

'Get a little house somewhere,' I said. 'Mow the lawn'

I pictured myself sitting in a yard somewhere. Sun shining through the trees. Birds singing. 'Get a job,' I said.

'Yeah? Doing what?'

'I don't know. Maybe get back into magic somehow.' I nodded to myself as I thought about it. 'Something small and local. Pulling coins out of the air, making doves disappear.'

'A government killer turned kids' party entertainer?'

'Yeah, I probably wouldn't put that on the website.'

She smiled.

'So what about you?' I said. 'You always wanted to be a chef?'

'I kind of fell in it. When I left college, I decided to travel the world… see everything. Ended up working in restaurant kitchens to pay my way. Turned out I had some talent for it.'

'So how far around the world did you get?'

'Some way. I made it to Nepal. Climbed Everest.'

'You're kidding?'

'Not the peak, but… Base Camp.'

'You weren't tempted to try for the top? You strike me as that type.'

She smiled. 'No. No, it's too dangerous. It's like a graveyard up there, apparently. There's bodies in the ice that have been there for years.'

I nodded.

I then went still. Just stared at her – the words echoing through my head.

Bodies in the ice. It felt like room around me had disappeared.

'What?' she said.

I just gazed at her.

Alice sat at the edge of Lenny's mattress – Lenny eyeing me intently as he sipped at a glass of water.

'Think about it,' I said. 'Samantha Lederer disappeared in Gainsboro four years ago… which is why there's no missing persons reports for her now.'

I paced around the room as I tried to get it clear in my head. 'Lonos kills her. Maybe it's a sexual game that goes wrong, or maybe he's just into it. There's a gala on, people everywhere… so he buries her body beneath the cabin. But there's snow all year round there, it would have been perfectly preserved. Evidence, everything. And this PI is still looking for

173

her. The PI gets close to the truth… gets killed. A bomb destroys the cabin and everything to do with the girl.'

Alice eyed me dubiously. 'He's going to kill eight people just to hide the death of one?'

'He's not expecting the neighbors to be there. But if he can pin it all on Lenny, I doubt a psycho like Lonos is going to give a shit anyhow. All of a sudden it's about Will Jerome… no questions about who this girl might be, and he's home and dry.'

Lenny nodded to himself. 'He's got a thing for young girls, that's for sure.'

Alice chewed thoughtfully at her lip. 'You don't think it's coincidental that Will Jerome, my dad's most vocal critic, just happens to be staying at that same cabin where Lonos killed this girl?'

She was right about that. It was too neat. I don't know, maybe I was missing some connection, but something fitted here, I felt sure of it. Whoever killed that PI was the person behind the cabin bombing.

Alice's phone rang. Lenny stared at the number, then answered it.

'Yeah,' he said. He paused a moment. 'Where? Yeah, Atlantic Boulevard, I know it. How much?' The anger glowed behind his eyes as he listened. 'Just get it ready.'

He hung up. 'We got a boat out of Key West at one tomorrow morning.'

'You trust this guy?' I said.

'He's got no love for Lonos, I know that much.'

He scribbled the address down on a scrap of paper –

Carolands House, Atlantic Boulevard – then glanced at Alice. 'But he wants two hundred grand… all up front. I've got plenty of cash on the other side, but getting hold of it now is going to be tricky.'

Alice shook her head. 'I don't have that kind of money.'

He eyed her uneasily.

'You do,' he said. 'I set up an account in your name, just in case something happened to me. It's clean, don't worry.'

She looked a little taken aback by this.

'You got your driver's license?' he said.

She nodded.

'Then you two go get the money. Miami Mutual Trust, Downtown. I'll stay here with Martin.'

I wasn't sure how happy I was leaving Martin here with him, but Miami was going to be a risky place for Alice right now.

I nodded.

10

The Miami Mutual Trust bank looked more like a hairdressers. Decked out in glossy orange and navy plastic, it was a million miles from the sturdy, stone monoliths of Wall Street. Then again, with the amount of plastic in it, Miami Mutual would probably still be floating around long after Wall Street had turned to dust.

I waited nervously in the main reception as Alice sat in an office with one of the bank staff. Twenty-five minutes so far, but I guess two hundred grand in cash was a tall order for anyone. As the office door opened I eyed Alice carefully. She was carrying a briefcase with her now. She politely shook hands with the woman from the bank, then made her way over to me.

'All good?' I said.

She nodded. 'Let's just get out of here.'

We exited the bank and headed for the parking lot. I glanced down at the briefcase. 'Two hundred?'

'Five,' she said.

I shot her a look.

'In case we need it,' she said.

'Exactly how much is in this account?'

She eyed me uneasily. 'A lot.'

I'd have said that was good news, but she didn't

look that comfortable about it at all – like instead of half a million, she was carting around a bag full of Ebola.

As we crossed the street, her phone rang. She glanced at the number, then shook her head. She showed me the phone.

Shit. It was Willard. Twenty-four hours – I still had time.

I answered the call. 'Yeah.'

'Michael,' he said. 'Where are you?'

'In the city.'

'I just landed in Miami. I need you to do something for me.'

'Listen, I think I may have a lead,' I said. 'Samantha Lederer… she disappeared in Gainsboro four years ago. I think she could be the unidentified girl at the cabin.'

He went quiet a moment.

'You may be right about this, Michael,' he said.

His response caught me a little off guard.

'You sent me details about this private investigator, Robert Plack,' he said. 'We haven't been able to get into his firm's files yet, but we intercepted two phone messages sent by his partner at the firm, William Harman. Harman's in Miami right now. I'm not sure, but by the sound of it, he has information on who killed Plack.'

I let this sink in for a moment. 'Plack's killer and the cabin bomber are the same person, Willard.'

The confusion then struck me. 'Why's he in Miami? Why hasn't he gone to the police?'

Willard took a deep breath. 'I think he may be trying to blackmail whoever's responsible.'

I went cold. 'The fucking idiot... he's going to get himself killed.'

'He's staying at the Weyland Hotel on Bayside.'

'I'm going now,'

'Michael... '

'What room number? If he's got information connecting Lonos to this, I need to get it. What room number?'

'I don't know... the message just said the Weyland Hotel.'

I hung up, grabbed Alice by the hand and ran for the car.

Alice held the briefcase tightly against her chest as I pulled the car to a halt in the parking lot of the Weyland Hotel. All marble pillars and stained glass windows, it was a smart-looking place, the doormen squeezed into brass-buttoned uniforms.

I nervously eyed the ebb and flow of guests at the hotel entrance, then glanced at Alice.

'You stay here,' I said.

She shook her head. 'We stay together. If this guy's waiting to do a deal with Lonos, I don't want to be stuck out here on my own.'

I held her look for a moment, then nodded. I grabbed Lenny's pistol from the glove compartment, slipped it into my pocket, then got out of the car. As Alice followed me toward the hotel reception, she kept the briefcase close to her. She took hold of my hand like we were a couple as we approached the doorman. He smiled graciously, then ushered us inside. I eyed the receptionist – a smart, red-cheeked guy in his thirties. A wedding ring on his finger. Chances are he was straight, which would make it easier for Alice to charm the room number out of him than it would be for me.

I glanced at Alice. 'Think you can get the number?'

She stared at the receptionist, getting the measure of him for a moment. She nodded.

As she headed over to him, I stared back at the parking lot, watching every car that pulled into the hotel. Mostly tourists – their sun-burnt faces indicating they hadn't been in town for long. As I eyed a black Mercedes pulling into the lot, Alice appeared at my side.

'417,' she said. 'It's a private bungalow overlooking the beach.'

I kept my eyes on the Mercedes until a guy in his eighties emerged from inside. Unless Lonos was hiring killers from the local Bingo hall, this guy wasn't going to be much of a threat. I took another quick look around, then turned and followed Alice out the rear hotel doors into the lush gardens that led down toward the beach.

We reached 417, a secluded Spanish-style bungalow with its own miniature swimming pool. Whoever this Harman guy was, he was doing OK by the look of it. I checked no one was nearby, then knocked on the door. No answer. I knocked again, then stepped over to the windows. The shutters were closed from the inside, but

179

through the narrow slats the quiet, shadowy room looked empty.

I tried to door again, but the bungalow was silent.

'We need to find housekeeping,' I said.

Alice glanced around the neighboring bungalows, then nodded toward one about a hundred feet away – a trolley stacked with towels and cleaning products pulled up at the main door.

I nodded at her. 'Give me a moment.'

I headed through the manicured palms toward the bungalow. As I eyed the trolley, a housekeeper in her forties emerged from the front door.

I smiled at her. 'Excuse me. Is this the way to the beach?'

She pointed toward a broken-paved pathway through the trees. 'This way, sir.'

I glanced at her master key hanging from a thin chain on her belt.

'And where do I get towels?' I said. I glanced at a pile of freshly-folded towels on the trolley. 'Can I just take a couple of these?'

Before she could answer, I grabbed one, sending the whole pile toppling to the ground.

'Shit, I'm sorry,' I said.

'It's fine, sir.'

As I bent down to pick them up, the dutiful housekeeper leaned down and joined me. As she grabbed the towels, I unclasped the tiny chain and slipped the master key into my pocket. I got to my feet, then reached for whatever cash I had. I may have stolen luxury cars for most of my adult life, but stealing from an everyday working woman wasn't much to be proud of. I grabbed a fifty-dollar bill and offered it to her.

'There's no need,' she said.

'Please,' I said and I placed the bill in her hand.

She nodded. 'Thank you, sir.'

I smiled apologetically, then turned and headed back to 417.

Alice was peering through the windows as I returned.

'Anything?' I said.

She shook her head. I made sure the housekeeper was out of sight, then slipped the master key into the lock. The door clicked open.

We stepped into a cool, shadowy room. A brown leather suitcase lay open on the sofa, its contents strewn across the floor – shaving equipment, shirts and jeans lying on the carpet. I checked the rest of the rooms, the shutters closed in all of them. The sound of the beach in the distance – waves and laughing children. As Alice headed over to the rear windows, I checked the master bedroom. It didn't look like the bed had been slept in. An empty briefcase lying open on the desk. Chargers plugged into the wall, but no laptop or phone anywhere. As I checked the desk drawers, Alice brushed up beside me, her voice little more than a whisper.

'Michael,' she said.

I kept searching the desk.

'Michael…'

I glanced up at her. She pointed to the door-frame of

the en-suite bathroom. A crimson smear on the otherwise spotless, white wood. I stepped away from the desk, then slowly reached for the pistol and screwed on the silencer. I headed over to the bathroom and pushed the door open.

I went still. A man's body lying in the bath. In his fifties. Smarty dressed. Gunshot wounds to the head – his thinning gray hair, matted with blood. I caught my breath, then glanced back at Alice standing motionless in the doorway. I carefully reached into the guy's jacket, and pulled out a wallet.

Driver's license. William Harman.

Shit.

'Don't touch anything,' I said.

'We need to get out of here.'

I nodded. Lonos' guys had already taken whatever information Harman had been trying to sell.

I grabbed a handful of tissues from the bathroom, headed back to the desk and started wiping my prints off every surface I'd touched. I picked up the briefcase with my forearms and started rubbing it clean. As I did, the case slipped and thudded to the floor. I picked it back up, then stared curiously at it for a moment. The brushed-velvet lining of the case had dislodged itself – the inner panel sitting at an ugly angle against the aluminum outer shell. I carefully wedged my fingernails around the edges of the panel and pulled it away.

Beneath it lay a thin pile of documents. Phone records, by the looks of it. Long lists of numbers and times. I picked them up and studied them. I wasn't sure if this was the information Harman had been trying to sell. If it was, then he'd either refused to give it to Lonos, or he'd had copies made. Either way, the records were important enough to hide away. As I tried to make sense of what I was looking at, a couple of handwritten notes on one of the pages leaped out at me. This was Robert Plack's cellphone data. I feverishly scanned the handwritten notes in the margins – Harman's analysis of the data. It seems that Plack's phone had stopped transmitting at 15:43 on February 12th. The impact of his fall is thought to have been the cause. However, at 15:45, a call was made by another phone at the same location.

The call was to Sunset Marina.

My heart stopped as I stared at Alice.

I struggled to get the words out.

'It was Lenny,' I said.

'What? What do you mean?'

I couldn't believe it.

'The cabin bombing,' I said. 'It was Lenny.'

The bastard had been playing me all this time.

She took a step away from me, then shook her head. 'No. It can't be.'

'A call was made to Sunset Marina just after Robert Plack died. It had to have been confirmation of the hit.'

'It's wrong.'

'Alice…'

'It's wrong!'

She started panting, gazing aimlessly around the room.

'He didn't kill that girl,' she said.

I stepped toward her. 'Alice, listen…'

'He didn't do it!'

I tried to keep my voice calm. 'Alice…'

'What about Will Jerome! You think it's just a coincidence he was there?'

'Maybe Lenny got lucky.'

'Don't be so fucking stupid!'

'Alice…'

'He didn't do it. He didn't kill her.'

I stayed quiet, but my differing opinion on his guilt was becoming evident to her. She glanced nervously at my pistol lying on the desk, then grabbed it and aimed it at me.

'You don't go near him,' she said.

'I'm not going to kill him, OK. But if he did this, he needs to be held to account for it.'

'It's the same thing! You get him arrested, he's dead in a week!'

'He might have killed all those people! Samantha Lederer…'

She blinked back her tears, then shook her head. 'You don't go near him.'

I reached for the gun. She stepped back and cocked the hammer. 'I mean it!'

The fire in her eyes, I stayed put. She secured the gun in her right hand, then reached for her phone. As she kept the barrel aimed at me, she dialed a number, her hands shaking.

'Lenny?' she said. 'Yeah. Yeah, I did. He's with me. Listen… there's something else.'

She started to cry. 'He's got phone records connecting you to the death of a private investigator in Gainsboro... all those people at the cabin.'

She dried her eyes as Lenny spoke.

'I know,' she said. 'I know! But he's got these records. He wants to come for you.'

She paused again and listened.

She nodded. 'Yeah. OK. We're at the Weyland Hotel. Room 417. I know. Quickly.'

She hung up and wiped her cheeks dry.

'We're going to wait here,' she said.

'For what?'

'Lie down on the floor.'

'What?'

'On the floor.'

I held her look.

'Do it!' Her finger trembling against the trigger. 'I mean it!'

She didn't look like she was in any stable shape to be holding a cocked pistol. I kept my eyes on her and slowly lay down on the carpet.

'What's going on, Alice?'

She stayed quiet – the gun shaking in her hand.

'Alice...'

'Shut up.'

She leaned back and rested herself against the wall in the corner.

'He's sending someone here?' I said. 'You're OK with that?'

She said nothing.

'He's going to have me killed too, Alice. He's going

to kill me.'

'You tried to kill him.'

'I didn't do it!'

Her tone turned bitter as she eyed me. 'What's your name? What is it, Rick? Michael? You're nothing but a liar and a thief. He's my dad!'

Shit, I was losing her here. As she kept the barrel aimed at me, I went quiet and I tried to think. Lenny may have lost his most loyal men but I had little doubt he knew plenty of local freelancers. The moment this guy showed up, I was fucked.

I eyed her intently. 'You can't do this, Alice. Think about Martin, for God's sake. You're not a killer.'

I kept my eyes on her, then slowly began to lift myself from the floor. The bullet zipped passed my cheek and thudded into the carpet. I froze.

'Don't test me,' she said.

'Alice…'

'Get back down.'

I stayed put. She stepped forward and took aim at my head. Jesus, she'd never looked more like Lenny's daughter than she did right now.

She nodded. 'Do it.'

I lowered myself back onto the carpet. 'What's Martin going to think of you?'

'Don't you dare! We were fine until you showed up. This is your fault.'

'And the people at the cabin? Lenny doesn't have to answer for that, right?'

'You don't know what you're talking about.'

'You may not know him as well as you think.'

'You don't know him at all!'

She took a deep breath, then nodded to herself. 'We're going to be quiet now. We're just going to wait.'

'Alice…'

She shook her head.

'Alice!'

But she switched off, my pleas falling on stony ground.

The minutes ticked by. Silence in the room. Just the bright sound of children's voices playing out on the beach. I tried to engage her again, but it was useless. She just crouched down into the corner, her tired arms resting against her knees as she kept the pistol aimed at me.

As the waves rolled against the shore in the distance, there was a gentle knock at the bungalow door.

Alice nervously raised her eyes from me. 'Hello?'

A soft-sounding male voice from outside. 'I'm a friend of your father.'

Whoever this guy was, it hadn't taken him long to get here. Probably the same guy Lenny had sent to kill Harman.

'We're at the back,' said Alice.

Keeping me in her sights, she got to her feet. She headed over to the door overlooking the bungalow's garden and unlocked it. Footsteps on the stone path outside – my blood racing as an ashen-faced guy in his forties appeared at the bedroom window. He eyed us a moment, then calmly stepped into the room. A weak shadow of a guy, his scrawny frame hardly filled the cheap brown suit that hung from his shoulders. He looked more like an accountant than a hitman.

'You're Alice?' he said.

She nodded.

He produced a pair of leather gloves from jacket pocket and pulled them on. 'Is this the man?'

She nodded again.

He gestured toward her gun. 'Can I have the gun, please?'

He calmly took it from her, placed it in his jacket, then took out a large, silver, silenced pistol.

'I'm to take care of this, then drive you to your father,' he said. 'Could you wait in the other room, please?'

She gazed at me a moment.

I held her look. 'Alice… don't do this.'

She closed her eyes a moment, then stepped out into the living room. The accountant held the pistol on me as he closed the door behind her. My heart thumping against my chest, I glanced at the door to the garden. He hadn't locked it after he'd entered, but there was no way I'd make it.

'Head down, please,' he said.

I stared back at him.

'Please?' he repeated.

I stayed put.

He sighed. 'As you wish.'

He aimed the pistol at my forehead. I tried to keep my eyes open, but it was no use – I blinked them tightly closed.

The sudden, whispering sound of a silenced bullet. My heart stopped. The soft thud of a body falling to the carpet.

The sound of distant waves rolling onto the beach.

I opened my eyes to find the accountant lying on the bedroom floor beside me. Thick gouts of blood pouring from a hole just below his right eye.

A shadow in the sunlight – a figure standing in the garden doorway.

Willard.

He closed the door behind him as he stepped into the bedroom. 'Good afternoon, Michael. I take it things aren't going well.'

The sheer wonder in me to see him.

'Jesus... Willard.'

He nodded. 'You're welcome.'

I caught my breath, then hauled myself back up to my feet.

'How long have you been here?' I said.

'I just arrived... I followed him in.'

I took a deep breath and tried to calm myself.

'Where's Harman?' he said.

I nodded toward the bathroom. As he took a look at the body in the tub, I glanced at the accountant, the phone records lying scattered around him on the carpet.

I scooped up the pages, sighing to myself as I stared again at Harman's notes.

'You were right,' I said. 'It was Lenny.'

Willard shot me a look.

I handed the pages to him. 'Some guy phoned

Lenny just after Plack died… a hitman, most likely.'

'That's the evidence?' He took a quick look at the records. 'It's circumstantial at best.'

'Come on, what are the chances that some innocent friend of Lenny's was right beside the PI when he died?'

A noise from the living room next door. Willard raised his gun.

'It's fine,' I said. 'It's Lenny's daughter.'

'Is she armed?'

I shook my head, then headed over to the door. I opened it to find Alice standing by the window, her head bent low in the shadows. As Willard followed me out of the bedroom, she turned and gazed at us, a mixture of confusion and dread on her face.

'This is Willard,' I said. 'An associate of mine. This is Lenny's daughter, Alice.'

Silence as Willard stared at her.

'Where's Lenny?' he said.

She shook her head. 'Please… he didn't do it.'

'Where is he?' he repeated.

I glanced at him. 'It's fine, I know where he's hiding. I'll deal with it.'

The uncertainty in his eyes as he looked at me.

'I'll deal with it, Willard.'

I meant it. Lenny had murdered Samantha Lederer – all those people at the cabin – then tried to have me killed as well. All attempts at a civilized resolution to this had well and truly been kicked out of the fucking window. I should have just killed him at the tower.

Alice stepped forward. 'Martin…'

'Don't worry about Martin,' I said.

Willard reached out and grabbed her phone.

I turned to him. 'Lonos still wants them dead,' I said. 'There's a boat out of Key West at one in the morning... Carolands House, Atlantic Boulevard. Make sure she's on it.'

'No,' said Alice.

'I'll bring Martin, don't worry!'

I eyed her uneasily, then took her by the arm.

As gently as we could, Willard and I escorted her out of the bungalow toward the hotel parking lot. Willard kept his eyes fixed on her but she didn't make a sound. What was she going to do, call out for security? For the police? With Lonos baying for blood, and Martin still out there, that was going to be a bad move.

We approached Willard's rental car gleaming in the parking lot. A run-of-the-mill Toyota Camry, it may not have been the vintage Mustang that normally signaled his presence, but it suited him a lot better. He opened the passenger door and ushered Alice inside.

As she climbed into the car she gazed at me, searching my eyes for assurance. 'Please, bring Martin.'

I nodded. 'You'll see him tonight, I promise.'

'And my dad?'

I wasn't going to lie to her. I stayed quiet. As she kept her eyes on me, Willard gently closed the car door.

He glanced back at the hotel. 'If that seedy little hitman doesn't report in, Lenny's going to get suspicious.'

I shook my head. 'He's hurt. His grandson's with him. He's not going anywhere.'

'Are you sure you don't want me to take care of it?'

I shook my head.

He handed me Alice's phone. 'Call me the moment it's done.'

I nodded. 'Just get her to Key West.'

11

I drove back toward the Glades, the heat pouring down like anger from the sun. As the road shimmered ahead of me, I pictured the quiet house where Lenny and Martin would be waiting: Martin, for his mother, and Lenny, for news that I was dead. I glanced at Alice's phone on the passenger seat as it rang again – the ninth or tenth time in the past hour. Lenny calling from the house, no doubt, to find out what had happened. I let the call ring out, and tried to steel myself. I didn't know if I had what it would take to kill him in cold blood, certainly not in front of Martin. If we'd found just one more piece of evidence – something less circumstantial – I might have been be able to wriggle out of having to do this. I might have been able to convince Southwest to hand it over to the courts. But it was too late for that. I needed to stay strong now. Focused. I needed to finally finish the job that I'd been sent to do.

Willard was going to arrange a DNA test to confirm that Samantha Lederer was the unidentified woman at the cabin. I had little doubt the results would come back positive. But the question still itched at me. Lenny may have been responsible for her death, but what the hell had Will Jerome been doing at the exact

193

same cabin, four years later? It couldn't have just been a coincidence. Unless Jerome was part of it, maybe. Maybe he and Lenny were both responsible for her death – Jerome heading back to the cabin in a bid to move the body before it was found. But then why the bomb? Unless Lenny decided that Jerome had to be removed too. The problem was I didn't buy any of that for a second. Jerome just didn't fit the profile.

As I rolled the possibilities around in my head, I sat upright at the wheel, a moment of clarity crystallizing in me. Jerome may not have been involved, but there was a detail to that scenario that made sense. Lenny would have tried to move the body at some point. When he murdered her, the cabin may have been the only option for him. But her body was buried under an occupied residence. It wasn't exactly the most secure of places, not for that period of time. He'd probably have had his people go back to move it – certainly if he'd found out there was a PI sniffing around. There might be records of his guys renting the cabin in order to do so. Shit, there might even be records that Lenny had been there in the first place.

I grabbed the phone and pulled up the case details on the Southwest site. The couple who'd owned the cabin, Jonathon and Louise McRae, died in the blast. But among the people that the police had interviewed was Louise's sister, Janet. I stared at her details – her phone number in New York.

I dialed the number and waited, praying for any kind of lead, anything that might provide a stay of execution.

A woman's voice picked up the call. 'Hello?'

'Janet McRae?' I said.

'That's right.'

'Hi, my name's Rick Sullivan, I'm a journalist looking into the Oregon bombing. Would you mind if I asked you a few questions?'

The chirpiness in her voice faded. 'I've really got nothing else to say about this.'

'I'm sure. It's just a couple of outstanding queries I thought you might be able to help me with.'

She paused uneasily. 'What queries?'

'Your sister and her husband lived in the cabin, right?'

'That's right.'

'When did they first buy the place?'

'Er... about eight years ago.'

'And they rented it out.'

'Occasionally, during the summer. But they stopped after Jonathon retired.'

'When was that?'

'About three... nearly four years ago.'

Soon after Samantha Lederer's death. 'Do they have records of who they rented it to?'

'I don't know. If they did, they were destroyed in the blast.'

I sighed. Fuck, no record that Lenny had been there. I stared out of the windshield a moment, and tried to think. Jonathon McRae retires, then stops renting the cabin. If Lenny's guys had tried to move the body, how would they have gotten back in? Unlike planting a bomb which probably wouldn't have needed more than

195

a few minutes, removing a buried body would have taken some time.

'Did they ever have any remodeling work or maintenance done after Jonathon retired?' I asked.

'They never mentioned it. Why?'

'I'm trying to find out if anyone else had access to the cabin for any extended period of time. What about vacations? Did they ever visit family, anything like that?'

'We tended to visit them there… it was beautiful. They'd visit Jonathan's cousins in Maine occasionally, but they had friends who'd look after the cabin while they were gone. The place was rarely empty, if that's what you mean.'

The wind in my sails started to fade. 'And you're sure they never rented it out again?'

'I don't think so. Jonathon got an offer a couple of years ago, a huge offer. He still wasn't interested.'

I slowed the car a little.

'What do you mean a huge offer?' I said. 'What offer?'

'Some man turned up, offered Jonathon ten thousand dollars for one weekend.'

'One weekend? Who?'

'I don't know. All Jonathon said was this man turned up with a lot cash.'

My heart jumped a gear.

'Did he give you any kind of description of the guy?' I said.

'Not really. Just that he was rich, that's all.'

'He didn't mention his age, appearance, anything?'

'No.'

'Please, try to think. It doesn't matter how small the detail.'

'Really, he just mentioned it in passing. Why?'

'Where did they meet, at the cabin?'

Her tone turned edgy. 'I don't know.'

Fuck. This was our guy, I was sure of it. Who offers ten grand for one weekend at a cabin? It wasn't some palace in Monaco. My mind raced as I tried to get a handle on it. It would have to have been one of Lenny's most trusted men – Cole or Paddy maybe.

'Might your husband know anything else about this?' I said.

'My husband?'

'Jonathon might have mentioned some detail to him.'

She sighed irritably. 'I'm sorry, Mr. Sullivan, but I'm done answering your questions.'

'Please, just...'

'I'm sorry. Good bye.'

My heart sank as she hung up.

I stared at the phone, my finger hovering over the redial button. But I was clutching at straws here – and desperately so. This was less about proving Lenny did it, and more about getting me off the hook. Shit, even if it had been Lenny himself who'd offered ten grand for the cabin, that probably wouldn't prove anything in court either.

There was no escaping this.

I took a deep breath, then gazed out at the highway. The mangroves rising out of the haze signaled the house was only a few short miles away now. Whoever this mystery man at the cabin may have been, I was out of time. I glanced uneasily at the glove compartment, then reached inside and grabbed the pistol. I might have wanted to avoid shooting Lenny in cold blood, but chances are I'd now be shooting in self-defense. He was going to know something had happened to Alice by now. The moment he realized it was me entering the house, things were going to get bad for sure. I checked the clip, then slipped it into my jacket pocket.

I pulled into the quiet neighborhood, the scattered buildings sitting within the trees like an old frontier town. I stopped the car a couple of streets away from the house, and switched off the phone – I didn't want another call from Lenny signaling my arrival. I eyed the house through the branches. A shady stillness through the windows. Lenny would probably be watching the front – he might even have told Martin to watch the back. I glanced around the empty streets, then got out of the car. I secured the gun in my belt, and crept through the brushwood toward the backyard. Cicadas chirped in the heat as I slipped behind a twisted oak at the edge of the yard. I stared carefully at the windows trying to make out any movement in the house. A tiny grass snake winding through the dry scrub beside me. I gazed at the upper windows, but the reflections remained still.

I grabbed a small stone from the ground, measured its weight, then tossed it at the roof of the rear porch. It landed on the tin tiles, clattering as it bounced into the gutter.

No sound. No movement. Nothing.

The pistol gripped firmly in my hand, I eyed the porch. The rear door sitting in the shade of the overhang. I darted away from the tree, across the lawn, then slowed to a crawl as my feet hit the wooden porch decking. I calmed my breathing and glanced through the main window. The living room looked empty, nothing stirring in the shadowy room. I eyed the tiny glass panel in the door that I'd broken last night. I reached through the hole, unlocked the door, and silently spun inside. My heart raced as I scanned the corners. I held the pistol in front of me, listening carefully as I stepped toward the staircase.

I went still. A sound from upstairs.

Crying.

I leaned my head around the base of the staircase, a floorboard creaking under my weight. As I shifted my foot, a figure appeared at the top of the stairs. Martin. Tears in his eyes as stared down at me.

'Go away,' he said.

'Martin,' I whispered.

'Go away.'

'Are you OK?'

He wiped his face. 'Please.'

I kept my eyes on him as I slowly climbed the stairs. I reached the upper landing, Martin standing firm as he tried to block my path. I peered into the bedroom. Lenny was lying on the mattress. His face, pale. His lips, cracked and dry. Only the faintest movement in his chest as he struggled to breathe.

I eyed Martin a moment, then gently ushered him to one side.

'Please don't hurt him,' he said.

I headed into the bedroom, and stared at Lenny's hands: a pistol in one, the house phone resting in the weak, uncurled fingers of the other. I headed over to the bed, removed the pistol from his hand, and slipped it into my jacket pocket.

He opened his eyes and tried to focus. However sick he may have felt, the look on his face sank even further as he realized who was in the room.

'What did you do to her?' he said.

'She's safe,' I replied.

I turned to Martin. 'Your mom's safe.'

'Where is she?' said Lenny.

'With a friend of mine.'

Lenny eyed me for a moment, then coughed weakly.

'Here for me, are you?' he said.

I glanced at Martin. 'Go to your room, I need to speak to your grandpa.'

Martin shook his head.

'It's going to be fine,' I said. 'Martin? Please.'

He stared at the gun in my hand. I slid it away into my jacket. I wasn't going to need it. Lenny didn't look like he was going to make it to the end of the day.

'Please?' I said to Martin.

Lenny raised his head. 'It's fine, Martin. Go to your room.'

He waved a hand for him to go. Martin eyed him

nervously a moment. As he slowly stepped next door, I closed the door behind him. I pulled up a chair and sat down beside the bed, Lenny reaching for breath as he watched me.

I held his look.

'I know it was you,' I said. 'The bombing... the PI... the girl at the cabin.'

'Would it make any difference if I said you were wrong?'

'Why did you kill her? Samantha Lederer?'

'I didn't.'

I gritted my teeth. I wanted to hear it from him. I needed to silence those last, lingering doubts in me.

I glanced out of the bedroom window at the leaves glistening in the sunlight. The branches bending lazily in the breeze.

'You believe in God, Lenny?'

He chuckled to himself. 'A Godless universe could never have made us. It takes something genuinely stupid for that.'

He laid his head back on the pillow, then wiped the sweat from his eyes – his hand falling weakly against the mattress.

Silence as he lay there. Just the trees rustling in the breeze.

'What are you waiting for?' he said. He glanced at me, then shook his head. 'Worst fucking hitman I've ever seen.'

'I'm taking Martin and Alice to Key West,' I said.

'Good.'

He strained to reach for the scrap of paper he'd

noted the address down on.

I nodded. 'It's fine, Carolands House, Atlantic Boulevard, I've got it.'

He sank back onto the pillow. 'The guy's called Bodie. Give him the money, he'll be fine.' He licked at his cracked lips. 'You'll make sure they get out?'

I nodded.

As he caught his breath, he gazed into the distance.

'He's all that matters to me, you know,' he said. 'Martin. I've never been scared of anything my whole life. But the moment he turned up with Alice... the moment I realized who they were. I was terrified.'

He glanced at me. 'You got kids?'

I shook my head.

'Fear like nothing else,' he said.

'Tell me why you did it, Lenny.'

He closed his eyes.

'I've got phone records that...'

'You've got nothing! Obviously! It wasn't me.'

His body shuddered as he coughed. 'Not that it fucking matters now.'

'I need to know, Lenny.'

He laughed again. 'Honestly... worst ever.'

'You're going to die, you understand? Tell me it was you, and I'll do what I can... get you to a doctor...'

'Oh, stop.'

He leaned toward the edge of the bed, then reached out a hand and took hold of my arm. The conviction in his eyes as he stared at me.

'I'm not having my grandson think that of me,' he

said.

He held my look a moment, then let go of me and rolled back onto the pillow.

'Maybe this is how it has to be,' he said. 'Maybe Emilio has to take over.'

He gazed back out of the window. 'You know, when I was growing up, the Italians still ran my neighborhood. You could deal with them, you know. There were some mean ones… but most of them were just talkers. Italians like to make threats, you know… horse's heads, dead fish. When Al Capone died I bet he was more scared of the pets he'd run into in the afterlife than the people. But the Mexicans… Mexicans are different. They'll kill anybody. For anything. It's a new world. I'm too soft for it now.'

He glanced at me. 'Like you. You won't last in this business. You care… it's no good.' He nodded to himself, then glanced at the door. 'Go check he's OK.'

I kept my eyes on him. He might have been playing me, but the voices in me that spoke Lonos' name were gaining strength again. I felt lost.

I sighed, then got to my feet and headed for the bedroom door.

'Be gentle with him,' he said. 'He thinks you're here to kill me. Some hope of that, huh?'

I headed out onto the landing and into the neighboring room. Martin was sitting cross-legged on the floor. As I knelt down in front of him, he stared at me, a look in his eyes like I was a ghost.

'I didn't hurt him, OK?' I said. 'But he's sick. I'm going to take you to your mom.'

203

'We can't leave him.'

'I need to get you guys out.'

A sound from outside – the clunk of a car door in the distance. I headed over to window and checked. The road looked quiet, just a family saloon pulling away beyond the trees.

I glanced back at Martin. 'It's going to be fine.'

He eyed me uneasily.

'I did something bad,' he said. 'I thought you were going to hurt him.'

'I'm not. I told you.'

He stared down at his hands, then toward the phone on the bedside table

'I called the police,' he said.

I gazed at him for a second.

'He wouldn't wake up,' he said. 'He said you were going to come for him now. I didn't know what to do.'

My heartbeat faded. 'When?'

'I don't know… an hour ago.'

'Did you tell them your name? Lenny's?'

He nodded.

I closed my eyes. 'Martin, you shouldn't have done that.'

'I was scared.'

Fuck.

More noises from outside. As I stepped back to the window, I caught a glimpse of a long shadow disappearing behind one of the neighboring houses. I gazed down the street – movement beyond the branches.

My heart thumping against my chest, I gazed back

at Martin, then grabbed him off the floor.

I hushed him. 'Quiet.'

I hurried him out of the bedroom and back into Lenny's room.

'Lonos' guys are here,' I said.

Lenny raised his head from the pillow.

Footsteps running down the side of the house. Muffled voices. I stared at the porch roof just below the bedroom window.

'Give me a gun,' said Lenny.

The downstairs door creaking open. I put down Martin, grabbed my gun, then ran over to the staircase. A figure standing at the bottom holding an automatic weapon. Before I could raise my gun, a cracking sound split the air. I collapsed onto the landing – the bullet tearing at my head. My body lying useless on the floorboards. Blood blurring my vision. I tried to move as the footsteps clambered up the stairs. But it was no use.

Martin's screams faded to an echo as everything went black.

12

Intense heat.

Burning.

I tried to move my head. It was like trying to twist a rusty faucet.

I forced my eyes open. Everything a blur. The air glowing orange around me. Fire.

I raised my head off the floor, my hair stuck to a pool of dried blood on the boards. The pain like acid in my veins. I felt at the wound just above my right ear, a soft tear in the flesh that stabbed as I ran my fingers across it. I tried to get to my feet – my heart racing, my body wavering like it was balancing on ice.

Fire raging downstairs, flames licking up the stairwell. As smoke billowed up against the landing ceiling, I staggered back into the bedroom.

'Martin! Martin!'

I checked the neighboring room. The place was empty. No sign of Martin or Lenny.

'Martin!'

Fuck, they had him. My heartbeat hollowed to nothing.

I tried to focus on my wristwatch. I didn't know how long I'd been out. 4:20 p.m. As the flames tore up the staircase, I stared back at the bedroom window –

the glass, shattered. I stumbled over to it and eyed the porch roof below the window. Flames engulfing the beams beneath it. As the bedroom door ignited behind me, I leaned my body out the window and tumbled like a loose sack of sticks onto the searing tin roof, the beams and tiles collapsing under my weight. I thudded into the front yard, burning wood and splintered glass beneath me. The house like a roaring furnace beside me, I heaved myself to my feet, cleared the front yard, then staggered down the street. An aging woman watching from the window of a neighboring house. Sirens in the distance. I couldn't stop, couldn't risk be held. I needed to get to Martin.

I climbed into the car and checked my jacket – Lenny's pistol lying safely in the pocket. I winced as I started the car, my vision a sweating blur as I pulled out onto the road.

Alice's phone on the passenger seat. I grabbed it and dialed Willard's number.

The call rang. No answer.

'Come on...'

The answering service clicked into life.

'Willard... leave Alice at the Key and get to Lonos' house as soon as you can. They took Martin. Bring whoever you can with you.'

I slipped the phone into my pocket, and hit the accelerator.

As the roads skimmed past the car, images of Martin ran through me – a demonic collage of blood and tears. Lonos' eyes looming through it all. I tried to keep a grip on myself, but the fear in me was running untamed. Lonos' men had taken Lenny too, which meant only one thing: they were intent on seeing him suffer. They'd make him watch Martin die.

My hands shook against the wheel as I raced toward the coast. The palm trees hanging against a violet sky, the sun melting gold into the ocean. A picturesque landscape that looked dark and twisted to me now. I cursed myself, my stupidity. From the very beginning, my instincts had leaned toward Lenny's innocence in all this. I didn't give a damn about the phone records, they could have come from anywhere. Print-outs that any one of Lonos' guys could have put together. I hadn't checked them, I just let the anger in me take over. And now Martin was going to pay for it. I floored the pedal – ninety miles an hour, a hundred – and prayed there was still time.

I cleared the highway, then weaved my way through the lush, palm-lined roads of Key Largo. I pictured Lonos' house sitting on its own in a quiet bay at the southern end of the island. I couldn't remember the address, but as I followed the coastal road, I recognized the colonial-style houses that we'd passed as Danny had driven me here. The bleached wooden edifices began to disappear as the road wound south. Just trees now – the beach flickering through the branches as I sped on. As the road arced across a sandy hill, I caught sight of the beach, and pulled the car to a stop.

I gazed down at the winding coast. There it was, maybe half a mile away – a prism-like house glinting in the sun. The kind of secluded palace that could only be paid for in blood. I eyed the armed guard by the main gate, then scanned the rest of the compound. No one else visible. The air, still. The guard at the gate, texting on his phone. I didn't like it – it was too quiet. There'd been a whole group of guards when Danny brought me here, but only one today. From my vantage point on the road I could see straight into the house. The drapes, open – the rear pool clearly visible through the rear windows. A second guard appeared beside the pool, a faded jade figure through the layers of glass. As he strolled aimlessly by the pool, my heart sank. Lonos wasn't here.

I gazed back at the guard by the main gate. He'd know where Lonos was. I kept my eyes on him, and tried to figure out the best play. There was no time for subtlety here – he had an automatic weapon that he'd have aimed at me long before I got anywhere near him. I could drive into him, maybe – try to wound him, get him to talk. But the guard inside would be on us in seconds. I couldn't think straight, the minutes ticking by. I had to move. Fuck it, I'd just drive and hope the cards fell my way. I started up the car, then reached for Lenny's gun resting in my pocket. As I did, I slowed. I went still. A roar in the distance, way behind me. The distinctive, melodic grind of a V12. I gazed out the rear of the car. Heading up the coastal road was Danny's black Lamborghini. I eyed it intently for a moment, then slowly swung the car around and cruised back down the hill. My eyes fixed on the fast approaching car, I reached for my seat-belt and buckled it firmly into the socket. A Chevy Silverado versus a Lamborghini Aventador. He may have had the speed but I had good old-fashioned American weight. As Danny zipped toward me, I got a clear glimpse of him through the sleek windshield. Two hundred feet away. A hundred. Fifty. He glanced at the Silverado – at me – his expression swinging from curiosity to shock. I floored the pedal, swerved across the lane and smashed headlong into the left wing of the car. The airbag exploded in front of me, my body lunging forward as the cars devolved into a single mess of twisting metal. The daze of the impact – the sudden, hideous compression. The Silverado rolled onto its side, juddering toward the beach before thudding to a halt against the trees.

The twisted creaking of plastic and metal. My body pressed up against the driver's window. The cracked windshield in front of me. Dazed, I reached a hand down the side of the seat and undid the seat-belt. I edged myself around, raised my legs, then kicked the windshield out – the urgency running through my veins. I crawled out of the car, the Chevy's wheels still spinning in the air behind me. I rose unsteadily to my feet, then stared back at the Aventador lying crushed on the other side of the road like some giant black cockroach. I grabbed the gun from my jacket and staggered over to it.

Danny lay motionless in the seat. I tugged at the smoking, twisted metal of the driver's door. Instead of rising gracefully into the air, it just fell off. I reached inside, grabbed Danny and pulled him out onto the road.

'Wake up!' I said. I slapped him 'Wake up!'

He stirred a moment – his eyes struggling to open.

'Where's Emilio?' I said.

Blood pouring from a gash in his forehead, he tried to focus on me. I grabbed him by his shirt collar.

'Emilio!' I said. 'Where is he?'

He licked at his lips – the tears in his eyes welling-up with pain. Anger.

'You're fucking dead,' he said.

'Yeah, yeah. Where is he?'

He spat at me. 'You're dead!'

I slapped him again. 'Danny… where's Martin?'

He fought back his tears. 'Emilio's going to make you pay for this.'

I aimed the pistol at him. 'I mean it!'

He stayed quiet.

'The kid has nothing to do with this!' I said. 'This isn't you! You want this on your head?'

'Fuck you. I didn't do nothing!'

'Listen to me, you're in a bad way here. You might make it… but it ain't going to be much use to you if you can't walk.' I pressed the pistol barrel against his right kneecap. 'Where's Martin?'

'I don't know!'

I cocked the hammer of the gun.

'I don't know!' he yelled. 'Emilio called.,.. told me to go to the house, just wait for him there.'

I glanced down the road – a car approaching. I stared nervously at it as it began to slow to a halt by the wreckage of the Silverado. A guy in his forties leaned out of the window like he wanted to help. As he stared at me, I straightened myself up and shook my head at him. He caught sight of the gun in my hand, then hit the accelerator and sped on by.

I pressed the barrel of the gun back against Danny's knee. 'You need to tell me where he is now.'

He closed his eyes. 'I don't know, I swear.'

I eyed him intently. But I knew him, it sounded like he was telling the truth. Fuck. I tried to think. If Lonos was with Martin and Lenny, it would need to be somewhere secluded. Quiet. Somewhere where he could play out his little revenge fantasy without any fear of interruption.

'What buildings does he own?' I asked. 'Something remote, empty.'

'I… I don't know,' he said.

'Think!'

'I don't know his whole operation.'

'Where would he go!'

'He… he has an apartment on Palm Beach.'

I shook my head. 'Where does he work from?'

His eyes flickered a moment.

'He owns a warehouse,' he said.

'Where?'

'In Miami,' he said. 'It's quiet. He keeps girls there sometimes.'

'Where?' I said.

'Wynwood. Sytes warehouse.'

'What's the set-up?'

'But they know who you are. They'll kill you before you ever get in.'

I'd worry about that later. 'What's the set-up!'

He struggled to think. 'I don't know… if Emilio's there, there'll be five or six guys at the main door.'

'What about other entrances? Windows?'

He shook his head. 'It's an old brick warehouse. There's a parking bay at the back, but you need the key… only Emilio and Rico have it.'

'Rico?'

'With the nose.'

I nodded – the flat-faced guy, the boxer.

'But they know you,' he said. 'You'll never get near them.'

I straightened myself up, keeping the gun aimed at his chest.

'I don't want to kill you, Danny. But you call Emilio…'

'I won't.'

'Believe me, I'll come back for you.'

'I won't!' he said. 'I didn't know about the kid, Michael! I swear. I don't want this.'

I held his look.

'I won't,' he said.

I don't know if I believed him, but this was as good as I was going to get. I couldn't shoot him in cold blood, I knew that. I took a deep breath. Sytes Warehouse, Miami. I glanced at the wrecked cars. The Lamborghini was toast and the Chevy didn't look much better. I stared back down the road – another car way off in the distance. I eyed it carefully. A silver pick-up. As it approached the hill I ducked low and laid myself down in the middle of the road. I kept my eyes half open as the pick-up climbed the hill. It slowed to halt about twenty feet from me, a confederate bumper sticker at the front. Two guys inside. Heavy-looking, the kind who could easily be armed. I didn't want to risk pulling the gun.

The driver got out. 'Damn!' he said.

On autopilot, he slipped the car key into his pocket, then ran over to me. 'Are you OK?'

I raised a hand, grabbed at his jacket, then nodded breathlessly toward Danny. 'My friend... please.'

As he and the other guy turned and headed for Danny, I palmed the car key. I waited a second while they checked on Danny, then got to my feet and quietly stepped into the pick-up. The guys turned back to face me, a look of confusion on their faces as I started the car, swung it round, then sped back down the road.

The sky was darkening as I hit the highway on the mainland, the pick-up's V8 straining under my foot. I tried to think straight, but I was a mess, physically and mentally. The wound in my head may have dried to a crust, but the pain was like a thick cloud around me, my blood pounding. I couldn't manage this on my own – I needed Willard's help. I grabbed the phone from my pocket: two missed calls from him.

I dialed his number. He answered immediately.

'Michael, what's happened?'

'They took Martin... I couldn't stop them. I'm heading for a warehouse in Wynwood. I think he's there.'

'What about Lenny?'

'He's finished.'

'What do you mean…'

'We need to get Martin!' I paused a moment. 'Have you told Alice?'

He sighed uneasily. 'She's… not good.'

Shit.

'Tell her I'm going to bring him to her,' I said.

'Listen to me, the police got the DNA tests back. You were right, it's Samantha Lederer.'

But I didn't give a shit now.

'I need you to leave Alice there,' I said. 'Meet me at Sytes Warehouse in Wynwood.'

'Michael…'

'Lonos' guys know me, I won't be able to get near them. You might be able to.'

He went quiet.

'We need to move now,' I said.

He took a deep breath.

'I understand your feelings about this,' he said. 'But I'm not prepared to take on Lonos' people.'

'Willard… '

'This isn't my job. It's not yours either! If you'd done what I asked of you initially, none of this would have happened! I'm not getting myself killed because you refuse to follow simple orders.'

'They're going to kill him!'

'He may already be dead.'

I shook my head. I couldn't think about that.

'I'm sorry,' he said. 'But I have a bigger picture to consider.'

I closed my eyes.

'I know this is hard for you, Michael, but… '

I hung up.

I laid the phone down on the passenger seat, and gazed out of the windshield. The fear in me that I wasn't going to be able get Martin out.

The dread in me that I was already too late.

13

The warehouses of Wynwood sat in the darkness like a collection of bad dreams. The blunt, rectangular buildings were covered in streams of screaming murals – wide-eyed faces painted onto the walls like each warehouse was on the verge of a nervous breakdown. The sky black above me, I stood by a shadowy line of spray-painted angels about three hundred feet from Sytes Warehouse. The colossal, redbrick structure filled the northern side of a large, open square; similar-sized warehouses lining the other sides. Its window cavities all bricked up, it had a particularly bleak, uninviting air about it – the word 'Sytes' painted in huge red letters across the front like a warning to the district. I stayed concealed in a narrow doorway just beyond the square and stared at the main entrance. A group of six guys stood huddled on the steps outside, their mood agitated but alert. No weapons visible, but their shirts and jackets sagged with the concealed metal beneath them. In the middle of the group stood Rico, the boxer – his flat face like a dark moon against the single caged light that lit the entrance.

Lonos was here.

As I gazed up at the warehouse, thoughts of what may be happening within its red walls boiled away in me. The urge in me to move – to try and shoot my way in – only just held in check by the undeniable futility of it. I eyed the side-street that ran down the eastern side of the warehouse. The luster of a closed roller-shutter in the brickwork – the parking bay. A security camera in the wall above it. As I studied the shutter, I focused on a small metal box in the brickwork beside it – the housing for the shutter controls, sealed with a padlock the size of my fist. I stared back at Rico and scanned the folds in his black, nylon track top looking for any sign of the key. I could make out the edges of a gun, but no indication of anything else. I looked him up and down. His pant pockets were empty, the keys had to be somewhere in the top. An inside pocket, maybe – but none of the folds suggested the weight. Either way, I wouldn't get within fifty feet of him before he recognized me. Fuck. If there'd been passers-by maybe I could have concealed myself within them and attempted some kind of approach. But the square was empty. The side streets, silent. Just the dull thud of dance music coming from one of the warehouses way off in the distance. The seconds ticking by, I gazed feverishly back at Rico, hoping some move would appear to me, some change to the status quo that I could exploit. Thoughts of Martin in that warehouse eating away at me. I couldn't just wait, I needed to do something. I eyed the warehouse roof, looking for anything that might suggest another access point – a skylight or air vent housing – not that I had any idea how I'd get up there. I peered at a loop of rubberized cable sagging just over the roof edge, then slowed a second.

I took my eyes off the warehouse and gazed into the darkness. Dance music coming from way behind me.

My heart slowed a moment. A nightclub.

I stepped out of the doorway and started running toward it.

Thick bass thumped through the walls of a corrugated metal warehouse two squares away. A buzz of people at the main door – a sparkling cacophony of glistening body-stockings and feather jackets. A sign above the entrance: *The Deep*. I took the pistol from my pocket, slid it behind a dumpster in the side-street, then headed for the entrance.

The security guys eyed me dubiously as I handed the cashier the entrance fee – my wounded, disheveled appearance raising no small amount of suspicion. As one of the guys patted me down for drugs and weapons, I kept my eyes on the crowds just beyond the foyer door.

'What happened to you?' said the security guy.

'I'm fine,' I replied. 'My friends are inside. I just need to see them for a minute, then I'm heading home.'

He stared uncertainly at me as he pondered my appearance, but I had no time for this. I grabbed a fifty-dollar bill from my pocket and handed it to him. 'Just five minutes. I won't be long.'

The guy kept his eyes on me a moment, then palmed the bill.

I cleared the foyer and darted into the heaving auditorium. Maybe a thousand people, thick masses undulating under the cascading light beams that filled the warehouse. Daft Punk pumping out of black speaker stacks in the ceiling. I surged into the sweating crowds and immediately started lifting – my fingers running delicately across bodies and bags like they were running scales on a piano. Wallets first. I needed an impressive-sounding amount of cash. A thousand dollars would do it. I slid through the sparkling dresses and gold jeans, chain-mail vests and taffeta blouses, dropping wallets and purses into my sagging shirt. As the shadows danced around me, I stopped a moment and gazed through the crowds. A group of Gothic-looking girls dancing under a burning spotlight near the stage. Their eyes like black pools against the snowy white make-up on their faces. The tallest of the girls, nearly six foot in her thigh-high boots, had a black leather handbag tied across her shoulder like an ammunition belt. I carefully eyed the bag's molded plastic zipper. As I pushed my way through the crowds toward her I folded my arms across my chest, my right hand hidden beneath my left elbow. She shot me an irritated look as I nudged passed her.

'I'm sorry,' I said, the fingers of my right hand unzipping the bag and trawling its contents up into my sleeve. As she continued dancing, I nodded politely, then slipped away into the crowds, my sleeve rattling with the plastic casings secreted inside.

The bathroom in the club's basement was quiet, just a couple of guys smoking weed by the door. I slipped into one of the cramped cubicles and started unpacking the wallets from my shirt. Maybe twenty-five of them.

I emptied the cash, counting out the crinkled bills into a pile on the toilet lid. A little over nine hundred dollars – that would be enough. They'd just take the money, no questions asked. I pocketed the cash, dumped the wallets in the trash, then emptied my sleeve of the items I'd lifted from the Gothic girl. A foundation stick. Mascara. Eyeliner. I headed out of the cubicle to the main mirror by the basins, then twisted open the foundation stick – a column of heavy white makeup rising from inside. I started pasting it onto my face, the thick streaks turning my complexion a bleached white – layer after layer until I looked like a radioactive albino. I grabbed the eyeliner, the soft black nib tugging at my skin as I quickly blackened my eyelids and sockets. I smeared the liner across my cheeks, shading deep black cavities beneath my cheek bones, then penciled rows of teeth across my whitened lips. As I blackened out the lower part of my nose, my features distorted into the harsh image of skull, the bloody wound on my head like a cosmetic flourish now.

The guys smoking weed by the door laughed. 'Zombie Boy,' said one of them.

I stared at my reflection. He was right. A bleached, blood-spattered skull sticking out of a torn black shirt. I looked like death at a wedding, like a cheap extra from a Bela Lugosi movie. But it was fashion, baby. More importantly, I doubted even Willard would recognize me. I kept my eyes on my reflection for a second, then raised a foot and kicked the mirror. It shattered into pieces, the shards chiming as they hit the floor.

'What the hell?' said the guy by the door.

I sifted through the shards until I found a jagged triangular piece about six inches long. I stood back up, holding the piece in my fist like a blade – the guys at the door disappearing instantly out of the bathroom. I slipped the shard up my sleeve then headed back into the club.

Thoughts of Martin streaming through me, I tried to stay focused. I darted back through the club's sweating crowds looking for any camouflage I could use on my approach. No matter how unrecognizable I may have looked to Lonos' guys, a guy on his own coming out of nowhere was still going to look suspicious. I needed to give them some kind of context they'd understand.

It didn't take me long to find it. Sitting at a booth by the main bar were a group of eight well-built guys in their early twenties. Suntanned pecs, Stetsons and mascara. Greek Gods, the lot of them, they looked like they'd just skied down a rainbow searching for adorable shoes. The main guy – a blue-eyed muscle boy in white velvet pants – was standing, shaking his hips to the music as he scanned the crowds. His friends drinking and laughing in the booth, I headed over to them and slapped the cash down onto the table.

'A thousand dollars to take the party outside for ten minutes,' I said.

Muscle boy threw me a look. 'What?'

His friends laughed like I was an idiot.

'A walk around the block,' I said. 'A thousand bucks.'

He raised his eyebrows at me. 'All we'll be doing is walking, huh? Fuck off.'

'It's not what you think,' I said. 'Just walk, that's it.'

He stared at his friends a moment.

'Why?' one of them said to me.

'Someone I'm trying to impress,' I said.

Muscle boy looked me up and down. 'The zombie look's a little last year, don't you think?'

I grabbed the cash from the table. 'You guys don't want to do it, I'll find somebody else.'

'Wait, wait, wait, wait…'

He eyed me carefully. 'A thousand bucks? Just to walk you around the block?'

I nodded.

'Are you OK?' he said.

'If you're not interested…'

He glanced back at his guys. They shrugged. Fuck it, there was eight of them and only one of me. As they grabbed the cash and slid out of the booth, I eyed a drink on the table, a plastic glass full of Coke with a single straw sticking out of the top. I grabbed it, then followed them out of the club.

My little parade of guys stayed quiet as I started leading them down the side streets toward Sytes Warehouse. But I needed noise. A party. Like none of us were trying to hide anything from anybody.

I took muscle boy to one side. 'What's your name?'

'David.'

'You sing?'

'Why, what do you like?'

'Anything. Just sing.'

He glanced at his friends, then shrugged.

They burst into song. 'We-are-fa-mi-ly!'

Yep, that would do it.

As they danced and sang, their mood relaxed a little. I subtly ducked away from them, reached behind the dumpster and retrieved my gun. I stuck it in the rear of my belt, then rejoined them, walking in the middle of the parade as we neared the square. Sytes Warehouse looming ahead of me, I handed David the glass of Coke, then nodded toward the side street that passed by the shuttered parking bay.

Leave this on the ground by those warehouse shutters,' I said.

'Why?'

'Just do it.'

The urgency in my voice now. He nodded.

Dancing like a Broadway chorus, we emerged into the square. Lonos' guys stared curiously at us from the main entrance. But no tension in their stance, no hands ready inside their jackets. They just watched, muttering jibes to each other.

I glanced at David. 'Keep going to the end of the street, then you're done. If you head back to the club, don't come back this way.'

'What's going on?'

'The guys outside the brick warehouse, are they looking at us?' I said.

He glanced over my shoulder. 'Yeah.'

'Then give me a hug.'

He laughed to himself, then threw his arms around

me.

'Good,' I said. 'Whatever happens now, you don't come for me, you don't help me. You understand?'

He eyed me curiously.

'I mean it,' I said. 'Just keep walking. Keep singing. No matter what.'

He nodded uneasily.

'Good,' I said. 'Go.'

I freed him from my arms, then turned and stared at Rico. My blood racing.

Showtime.

As the parade slowly sang its way across the square, I broke away from it and headed toward the main entrance. Rico's eyes fixed on me.

I opened my arms wide. 'Guys!' I said in my best British accent. 'Why so serious? We're having a party... come on!'

Rico rolled his eyes. 'Get lost.'

'Oh, be nice. Come on, some of you are cute.' I smiled at him. 'You, not so much. But we got whiskey and weed, come on.'

He laughed. 'Go fuck yourself.'

I slowed to a stop about forty feet from him. 'Your boyfriend know you talk like that?'

His eyes turned icy as he took a single step toward me. 'What the fuck did you say?'

I shrugged. 'But you got those big, soft lips... I bet he loves those, huh?'

He glanced at his guys a moment, then stormed down the warehouse steps. I scanned his pockets, the ripples in the material now that he was moving – but no indication of the key's position. I couldn't rely on blind luck, I was only going to get one shot at this. The panic rising in me as he got closer, no signs of weight anywhere in the track top. Fuck it, he was right-handed, I'd go with the right pocket. As he raised his arm to strike, the track top billowed in the air – the faint glint of metal beneath the material. My eyes widened as I caught sight of a slim set of keys clasped to a long, heavy chain around his neck.

'Faggot!' he said.

As I took a fearful step back from him I measured the key's position and readied myself for the impact. He swung his right fist at me. The punch landed – the pain rocketing through my skull. I spun under its weight, my left hand brushing against his body, releasing the key clasp from the chain. I clutched the keys firmly in my hand as I curled into a cowering ball on the ground, my ears ringing from the hit.

He kicked at my back. 'Bastard Judy Garland Motherfucker!'

The guys back on the steps began to laugh as he kept on kicking, the pain shooting through me. But the keys were in my hand and this idiot didn't have a clue what was going on. He could kick all he liked, I didn't give a shit.

He took a halting breath, then spat at me.

'Go tell that to your boyfriend,' he said.

He adjusted his collar like a show of victory, then headed back toward the entrance. I stayed on the ground a moment like the humbled foe that I was, then slowly got to my feet.

One of the other guys at the door threw me a look. 'You want some more?'

I eyed Rico, the chain hidden again beneath his half-zipped track top. As he glared at me, I bowed my head, turned and ran back across the square. I reached the corner of the warehouse and swung around it, my little parade of guys still singing as they disappeared past the buildings at the end of the side street.

I eyed the ground by the shutter, the glass of Coke resting by the warehouse wall. I scurried over, picked it up, then crept forward. Keeping myself out of sight of the security camera, I leaned my head toward the edge of the shutter and listened. A single set of footsteps shuffling around inside. A guy's voice cursing as a tinny digital theme drifted through the air. Whoever was on the other side of the shutter, it sounded like he was playing a game on his phone. I nodded to myself, then glanced up at the security camera. I sucked up a mouthful of Coke through the straw, aimed it at the camera lens, then fired a dripping stream of liquid at it. I doubted it would give me much cover, but all I'd need was a few blurry seconds. I dumped the glass, grabbed the keys, then quietly unlocked the shutter control box. Two large plastic buttons. I glanced nervously back at the square, then pressed 'open'. As the shutter rattled its ascent I let the mirrored glass shard slip from my sleeve into my fingers. I couldn't risk any gun shots alerting the guys at the main entrance.

A man's voice from inside the parking bay. 'Rico?'

I kept my head low to the camera and did my best

227

impersonation of a fucking retard. 'That's right.'

Silence from the other side of the shutter as it continued to rise. This guy wasn't buying it, but I could see his chest now, his arm reaching for a gun in his jacket.

'Rico?' he said again.

His neck appeared beneath the rising lip of the shutter. This wasn't going to be pleasant, but fuck it, they should never have taken Martin. I grabbed the glass shard firmly in my hand, darted under the shutter and stuck the shard deep into his throat. He tried to scream, kicking out as he grabbed at his gun. I held my left hand across his mouth, and dragged him down to the ground, his blood pumping into the air. As he kicked and grasped I wrapped my arms and legs around him, holding him tight as a parachute pack as I kept him subdued. He convulsed and fought, but as his blood spilled out into a thick pool across the floor, his efforts grew weaker – fading to nothing as the life finally drained from his body. My hands dripping, I released him, then got to my feet. I scanned the bay – two Range Rovers and an Escalade parked within the cramped concrete walls, a single closed door at the far end. I took a deep breath, then hit the inner control button. As the shutter rolled closed, I glanced down at the guy's body. A half-drawn, silenced pistol hanging from his shirt. I grabbed it and checked the clip. I had two guns now, and little doubt that I was going to need both of them. I blinked the sweat from my eyes, my heart pounding as I approached the parking bay door.

I leaned an ear to the door and listened. No voices

on the other side. Nothing. Keeping the gun squarely aimed, I carefully opened the door. A dark expanse ahead of me, maybe eight or nine thousand square feet. Piles of wooden packing crates dotted across the warehouse floor, the only light coming from the top of a staircase rising by the east wall. Searching for the slightest movement in the shadows, I crept through the towering crates until I reached the bottom of the staircase. I carefully leaned my head forward – a dull gray light in the ceiling of the next floor. Still no movement anywhere. But I could hear voices now. Indistinct. An urgency to them.

I edged up the stairs, scanning the upper floor as it came into view. The pale, low light cast muddy shadows across a row of stark, empty offices. Semi-opaque plastic sheets hanging from the ceiling serving as makeshift doors. I carefully pulled back a sheet and looked inside one of the offices. An empty room – just an old chair lying broken on the dusty concrete floor. As I let the plastic sheet swing back into place, I paused a second – a few strands of dried blonde hair stuck to the edge of the plastic. I spun round as one of the voices in the distance became clearer.

'We can't give him any more, it'll kill him,' came a man's voice. Weak-sounding. Elderly.

'I want him awake,' came the reply.

I went still. The second voice was Emilio's.

The elderly man continued. 'He's going into cardiac arrest... '

'You're the doctor. Do something. I want him awake!'

229

'I can give him another 30 milligrams of adrenaline, but… '

'Do whatever you fucking have to, just wake him up!'

I gazed down the corridor, my blood like ice. Movement and voices coming from a large office just ahead of me. I crept closer to the sheet that covered the entrance. Through the dusty plastic I could make out the blurry shapes of two men moving around.

The faint sound of tears.

I inched over and peered through the sliver of space between the plastic sheet and the wall.

Martin.

He was tied to a chair, arms behind his back. His head drooped forward, tears streaming as he kept his eyes tightly closed. I angled my view and caught sight of Lenny tied to a chair about ten feet from him, unconscious. The elderly guy knelt down beside Lenny and stuck a needle into his arm. As the guy stepped back, Lenny's head rolled drunkenly around on his shoulders.

I couldn't see Emilio, but I could hear him.

'Wake up, you fuck!' he said. 'Wake up!'

Lenny's mouth hung limp as his eyes slowly peeled open. He took an exhausted look at Martin, then licked his parched lips.

'Hello again,' said Emilio. 'Thought we'd lost you there for a moment.'

Lenny struggled to catch his breath – his voice, distant and weak.

'Don't do this,' he said 'I'll do anything you want.'

Emilio walked over to him – a glossy steel ax in his hand.

He grabbed Lenny's face. 'But this is what I want, Lenny. I want you to see it… the last thing you're ever going to witness on this miserable fucking planet.'

'Not the boy. Please. Not the boy.'

'Fine,' said Emilio. 'You bring me my father… I'll let the kid go.'

I peered as far as I could through the gap in the plastic, trying to get some read on the room. I couldn't see how many other guys were in there, but the ceiling lights cast the indistinct shadows of at least two more guys across the floor in front me.

Lenny rolled his head back and stared at Emilio. 'Your father was a piece of shit and you know it.'

Emilio slapped him.

Lenny kept on. 'If I hadn't killed him someone else would have.'

'But it was you, Lenny. Now we're going to settle the score.'

'You're going to rot in hell for this. You know that?'

Emilio shrugged. 'I've got seats booked there anyhow, so what the fuck.'

He scraped the tip of the ax against the floor as he dragged it toward Martin.

'Motherfucker!' said Lenny.

'Yeah, shush.'

As Emilio leaned down in front of Martin, I tried to get a better view of the guys behind Lenny. I tugged back the plastic a little and peered as best I could around the room – I still couldn't see them. Not that it mattered now, I was out of time.

Emilio ran a hand through Martin's hair – the poor boy crying his eyes out as Emilio raised his head to face him. As he did, Martin caught sight of me through the gap in the plastic. His eyes froze. God knows who he thought I was, but I raised a finger to my lips to hush him.

'I want you to think of this as a blessing,' Emilio said to him. 'You're only going to get old, get divorced, have a stroke... be fed through a fucking straw for the rest of your life. I'm doing you a favor here.'

My heart thumping like a stone, I raised the gun, then darted through the plastic – the automatic pistol shuddering in my hand it sprayed a thick stream of silenced bullets at three guys standing in the corner of the room. As two of them crumpled to the floor, the third reached for his gun and ducked behind Lenny. Emilio swung the ax at me. I dived to the floor, the blade ringing as it hit the concrete beside me. The guy behind Lenny took aim at me. I shot his ankles through the chair legs – his body collapsing to the floor, a single shot from his pistol zipping passed me. As Emilio took another swing at me, I rolled across the concrete and took another shot at the guy lying on the floor – the bullet hit him squarely in the face. I swung the gun around, looking for Emilio. He was gone – the plastic billowing in the air as I heard him racing for the staircase. I picked myself up, ran for the doorway, then fired again, the bullets erupting into dusty clouds in the brickwork as he disappeared down the stairs. I glanced back at Martin. Fuck. We wouldn't have more than a few seconds before Rico and his guys were on us. Lenny tried to focus on at me, a look of confusion on his face.

I ran over to Martin and leaned down in front of him. 'Martin… it's me. It's me! Are you OK?'

He gazed into my eyes.

I grabbed the ax from the floor and cut the duct tape holding him to the chair. 'We need to move.'

He stared at Lenny. 'Grandpa…'

'Go!' said Lenny. 'Get him out.'

I freed Martin, then ran over to Lenny and cut the tape from his hands.

'I'm not going to make it,' he said. 'Don't waste your time. Get him out.'

I hauled Lenny to his feet, swung one of his arms over my shoulder, then dragged him out of the office.

I glanced at Martin beside me. 'Stay close.'

I could already hear voices from inside. Emilio, Rico, the rest of them. Footsteps echoing through the warehouse – we'd never make it to the parking bay.

Lenny panted. 'Leave me. Just go.'

I gazed in desperation at Martin, then scanned the walls for any other way out – a window I might have missed, or fire escape. There didn't look to be anything that would take us down to street level. Beyond the offices, an open staircase rose up the north wall. I eyed it carefully. The roof was our only option.

'Hold on,' I said.

I grabbed Martin, then started heaving Lenny

toward the staircase, footsteps tearing up from the floor below us.

I nodded at Martin. 'Get in front of me.'

As Martin ran forward, I turned and fired a stream of bullets toward the lower staircase. I dragged Lenny as hard as I could, a volley of gunfire tearing passed us and sparking off the wrought iron struts in the ceiling. I took another shot back, the magazine clicking empty as I tugged at the trigger. I tossed the gun, then grabbed the pistol from my belt – a small automatic, eight or nine shots at best. I hauled Lenny to the base of the upper staircase, and stared up at the padlocked steel door in the roof. More gunshots behind us. I fired back again toward the offices, then lowered Lenny to the floor.

'I'm going to take Martin up,' I said. 'I'll come back down for you.'

As Lenny caught his breath, I ushered Martin behind me, took aim at the offices, then started climbing the open staircase. Bullets splintered into the brickwork beside us, Martin and I ducking low as I returned fire. I grabbed Martin in one arm and charged up to the door. The bullets from below came once again, the girders in the roof granting us a little cover as I shot at the padlock. The shackle ruptured. I kicked the door open, then pushed Martin outside.

'Don't move,' I said.

I stared back down the staircase, the gunshots turning the brickwork beside it to dust. As I fired again into the warehouse, Lenny gazed up at me from the lower steps.

'Don't,' he said.

Pistol barrels sparked by the offices, Lenny's body jolting as a stream of bullets caught him in the stomach.

Martin screamed. 'Grandpa!'

I held Martin back as he ran for the door. As he struggled in my arms, he stared down at Lenny lying against the staircase.

Lenny gazed back up at him.

'I love you, boy,' he said. 'I love you.'

'Grandpa!'

As Lenny fought for breath, a vague smile crept across his face. He glanced down, then slowly reached a trembling hand into his pocket. He produced a tiny stick of candy, winking at Martin as he began to twist away the wrapping.

He laughed. 'Hey… it's not so bad.'

Another stream of bullets tore into him. The candy fell from his hand as he collapsed limp against the stairs.

Martin stood there frozen, his eyes fixed on his grandfather. I grabbed him, pulled him out on to the roof and swung the door shut.

'Martin, listen to me! Martin!' I shook him back to attention. 'We need to leave! You stay close to me!'

He wasn't listening.

'Martin!'

I picked him up and ran for the loop of cable I'd seen hanging from the roof edge. A black cable, maybe forty feet long, it was connected to a satellite dish at one end, a junction box at the other. With the satellite dish looking more stable, I pulled the cable from the junction box, sparks flashing from the housing as I tossed the cable over the edge of the roof. I looked down, the end of the cable swinging ten or fifteen feet above the ground, the street empty. I held Martin tightly in one arm, the cable in the other, then launched myself over the edge. We slid toward the ground, the cable burning against my palm as I tried to slow us down. Twenty feet to the ground, fifteen – the cable then disappeared through my fingers. Martin landed on top of me as I thumped into the sidewalk. I couldn't breath, pain erupting through me. As footsteps raced across the roof way above us, Martin dragged me to my feet. He nodded toward a side street just ahead of us. Fire escapes and dumpsters. We tumbled toward them, ducking behind the iron and steel, the angels drifting past us as we ran for the car.

14

Martin sat silently in the car, the glow of the city fading in the rearview mirror as we headed south toward Key West. Toward his mother's arms and the boat that would take him far away from this. I wiped away the sweat-soaked remnants of my make-up against my sleeve, then glanced uneasily at him. He hadn't said a word since the warehouse. I didn't know what to say to him either. I was sorry Lenny had died. I was. But for Martin to have had to go through this? It was the worst.

I kept my eyes on him.

'You're safe,' I said. 'That's all he would have wanted.'

He stayed quiet.

I nodded. 'You'll be with your mom soon. It'll all be over.'

I glanced at the headlights in the rearview mirror and prayed that was the truth. It didn't look like we were being followed, but I had little doubt Lonos was spitting blood somewhere, trying to find us. I tried to think it through. The chances of him being able to track down our car were remote. A GMC pickup, it wouldn't have a tracker. It may have been reported stolen, but I doubted that finding it was going to be any kind of statewide emergency. No, the car was good. What concerned me was the address we were heading to. Carolands House, Atlantic Boulevard. I kept thinking about the scrap of paper Lenny had written it down on. The worry in me that Lonos' men might have found it when they stormed the house. I tried to picture the bedside table where Lenny had left it, the heat of the flames behind me as I'd stumbled in through the bedroom door. In my mind's eye the table looked empty. I don't know if I was being paranoid or not. It could have just fallen to the floor.

I kept my foot on the accelerator and I tried to stay positive. That the chances of Lonos having the address were remote too. Unfortunately, happy endings were an idea that had risen out of the exhaust fumes of fairy tales – and this was Florida.

I glanced down at a can of soda rattling around in the door compartment. I grabbed it, sparked it open and handed it to Martin.

'Here, drink something,' I said.

He didn't respond.

'Martin, come on. Please? You'll feel better."

He stayed still.

I placed the soda in the holder beside him, then glanced again at the rearview mirror.

His voice little more than a whisper. 'I didn't think you'd come.'

'Martin…'

His eyes welling up as he looked at me. 'I thought you were dead.'

I shook my head. 'I wouldn't leave you, Martin.'

I put an arm around his shoulders and hugged him close to me. He buried his head against my chest – and I felt as low as I could remember. I wanted to tell him how sorry I was. For everything.

I just held onto him.

It was past midnight by the time we reached the Keys, the Overseas Highway running like a silver thread across the ocean. Key West glittered softly in the distance as it rose out of the darkness. It looked like paradise, like a sea of possibilities lay beyond its southern shores. I eyed its restful lights, but whatever hope they promised washed passed me. We were near the rendezvous point now, and my nerves were rising again.

I kept my eyes sharp as we passed the palm-strewn beach houses on Atlantic Boulevard. Their windows, dark and sleepy. As I scanned the properties on the ocean side of the road, Martin sat upright in his seat. He pointed ahead of us to a tiny wooden sign by a secluded, tree-lined driveway: 'Carolands House'. I slowed the car to a stop, eyed the few cars that were parked nearby, then carefully scanned the driveway. It snaked into the darkness through a thick mess of palm trees. I tried to make out any movement in the shadows. No sign of anything, just leaves shimmering in the moonlight. I switched off the headlights, then cautiously turned onto the driveway. I kept my eyes on the shadows as we wound through the trees, the tires whispering against the tarmac. As we steered down toward the beach, the palms cleared ahead of us, revealing a large wooden house on a grass verge by the shore.

Secluded it may have been, but it didn't look like any drug dealer's house to me. All lace curtains and perfectly painted shutters, it looked like it had been designed by a bunch of Victorian nuns – like any moment Julie Andrews was going to appear at a window singing, 'Climb Ev'ry Mountain.' Beyond the palms on the ocean side, a wooden jetty stretched out into the water.

I eyed Willard's Toyota parked beside the house. No sign of him or Alice. I pulled the car to a stop and took another look around.

I glanced at Martin. 'We stay quiet.'

He nodded.

As we got out of the car I ushered him behind me, then searched the deep blue shadows that engulfed the house, the moonlight shimmering off the sea beyond it.

Willard's voice in the darkness. 'Michael.'

His silhouette emerged from the ocean side of the house. He glanced back at the house then nodded. Alice appeared in the shadows behind him. The moment she caught sight of Martin she ran toward him.

'Martin!'

He jumped into her arms. As she held him close and kissed him he started to cry.

'It's OK,' she whispered. 'It's OK.'

I just watched for a moment as they held each other, their reunion briefly dissolving the tension in me.

Willard stepped toward the dusty pick-up we'd

arrived in and scanned the inside.

'Where's Lenny?' he said.

I took a deep breath, then stared uneasily at Alice.

'I'm sorry,' I said.

Martin held back his tears. 'They shot him, Mom.'

She closed her eyes. As she held on tightly to Martin, Willard took me to one side.

'What happened?' he said.

The anger still simmering in me that he'd refused to help. 'It doesn't matter.'

He kept his eyes on me.

'He's dead,' I said. 'OK?'

He eyed me curiously – the smeared remains of white make-up on my face. He nodded to himself.

'You did well getting him out,' he said. 'What about Lonos?'

I shook my head. 'Still out there.'

I stared back up the driveway toward Atlantic Boulevard. A sense of movement all around me, the palm leaves rippling in the moonlight. I kept my eyes on the trees as a set of car headlights began to flicker through the branches in the distance. As the car rolled down the Boulevard toward the driveway, Willard reached for his pistol.

'I called in some back up,' he said. 'Klinger and Russo. It could be them.'

There weren't many houses this end of the Boulevard, the roads quiet. I kept my eyed fixed on the headlights, my blood racing as the beams slowly arced passed the driveway – the hum of the engine fading as the lights disappeared on through the trees.

I nodded toward the pistol in Willard's hand. 'Give me a gun.'

He eyed me a second, then headed over to the Toyota and popped the trunk. Strapped inside was an armored case. He reached inside and handed me a silenced, automatic pistol. As I checked the clip, he glanced back at Alice and Martin.

'Let's get inside,' he said.

The living room of the house was all embroidered cushions and tasseled, silk sofas. Nineteenth-century glitz. We kept the lights off as we waited by the bay windows, the sea glittering in the moonlight. Willard glanced back through the ghostly-lit room.

'I'll keep an eye on the driveway,' he said.

I nodded.

As he headed over to the other side of the room I checked my watch, then smiled reassuringly at Martin.

'The boat will be here soon,' I said.

He kept his eyes on me.

'Are you going to come with us?' he said.

The question took me by surprise.

'Martin…'

'Please?'

Alice stroked his hair. 'We'll be fine, sweetie.'

I took a deep breath, then knelt down in front of him.

'You and your mom need a fresh start,' I said. 'Away from all of this… people like me.'

'You're not like them though,' he said.

Alice kissed him on the forehead. 'We'll be fine

now.'

I paused a moment, then eyed him carefully.

'Listen to me,' I said. 'Your grandpa wasn't responsible for what happened in Oregon. I want you to know that. I don't want there to be any doubt in your mind.'

He nodded. 'I know.'

Alice stroked his cheek. 'Grandpa loved you more than anything.'

He eyed her tearfully again.

As he turned and stared back out at the sea, Willard's phone rang from across the room. Willard glanced at the number, then answered the call.

'Russo,' he said. He paused a moment, his demeanor tightening as he listened. 'How many? You're positive?'

He lowered the phone, then beckoned me over. 'Klinger and Russo, they've just reached the Key.'

He led me out of the living room into the hallway, then closed the door behind us. Alice and Martin out of earshot, he hit the speaker button on the phone.

'Michael Violet's on the line,' he said. 'Repeat the situation.'

Russo's voice over the speaker. 'There's two cars ahead of us... a Range Rover and an Escalade, both with Miami plates. Nine passengers between them. We've been on their tail for the last four minutes. They've just turned south onto Atlantic Boulevard.'

My heart jumped a gear as I gazed out at the driveway.

Willard spoke again into the phone. 'Give me the

243

plates, I'll run them.'

I shot him a look. 'We don't have time, Willard. It's them.'

I glanced anxiously back at the living room.

'Have you been identified?' said Willard.

'Negative,' said Russo.

'What's your weapons capability?'

'M4 Carbines. We can perform a drive-by if needed.'

He thought to himself a moment. 'Can you identify Emilio Lonos as a passenger?'

'No positive IDs on any of the passengers.'

I stared at Willard. 'It's them. They're going to be here in seconds. Give the order!'

He gazed nervously up at the trees that lined the Boulevard.

Russo's voice on the phone. 'Willard?'

He eyed me a second, then nodded. 'Take them out.'

'Confirmed,' came the reply.

I ran back into the living room and grabbed Alice and Martin.

'What's happening?' she said.

'Take Martin upstairs and lock yourself in one of the bedrooms.'

'What's happening!'

'Just do as I say!'

The fear in her eyes as she grabbed Martin by the hand and ran for the staircase. As they clambered upstairs, Willard and I stepped outside the front of the house, guns ready at our sides.

'There's fewer houses this end of the Boulevard,' said Willard. 'They'll wait til they get up here.'

I gazed up at the trees. It was anybody's call how this would pan out. Klinger and Russo were efficient agents – I'd heard their names at Southwest briefings – but they'd be up against nine well-armed gang members. We'd have surprise on our side but Lonos would have the firepower. I kept my eyes on the trees as I strained to make out any sounds in the darkness. Just the ocean lapping at the shore behind me. As I scanned the shadows, the distant hum of car engines began to rise in the air. I gazed up the Boulevard, the hum suddenly overtaken by the sound of screeching of tires. I held my breath as the clatter of high-speed gunfire erupted. A second later the trees' silhouettes took clear form as a fireball rose into the air behind them. About seven or eight hundred feet from us, the flames soared above the trees, gunshots ringing through the air again.

The gunfire then went quiet. Willard grabbed his phone. As orange-lit smoke began drifting through the trees, he dialed Russo's number and waited.

No answer.

My heart racing, I gazed at the flames glowing beyond the trees. Another burst of gunfire echoed across the Boulevard. Voices yelling in the distance, too indistinct to recognize. I stared back down the beach. The darkness of the shore might be a possible escape route for any of Lonos' men who'd survived. As I searched the shadows, I caught a hint of movement in the corner of my eye, way out to sea.

A sleek powerboat arcing through the moonlit water.

Gunfire crackling in the distance, I ran for the house, then burst through the front door. 'Alice! We're leaving!'

As I darted up the stairs, she appeared from one of the bedroom doors, Martin cowering behind her.

'What was that explosion?' she said.

'We're leaving! Now!'

I picked Martin up and ran back down the stairs, Alice following. I darted across the living room and out the ocean side of the house. As sporadic gunfire echoed again from the Boulevard, I kept Martin's head low against my chest and raced for the powerboat that was slowing to a crawl beside the jetty. Maybe seventy feet long, it looked like a silver dart in the water. Its sleek carbon-fiber roof-hatch slid back and a disheveled guy in his fifties stumbled out. He didn't exactly fill me with confidence – it looked like someone had pulled a Christmas cracker and an alcoholic had fallen out.

He stared nervously at the flames on the Boulevard. 'What the hell's going on?'

'You're Bodie?' I said.

He nodded. 'What's going on?'

'Get them out of here.'

He eyed Alice and Martin. 'You're Lenny's people? Where is he?'

'There's been a change of plan,' I said. 'Just get them out of here.'

He stared cautiously back up at the Boulevard, then

nodded. 'Yeah.'

I took Alice to one side, then lowered my voice. 'You got the money?'

She held tightly onto the bag on her shoulder.

'You don't pay him a cent until you arrive, you understand?' I said.

She nodded.

I reached for my gun and placed it in her bag.

'No,' she said.

'Alice…'

I couldn't have her and Martin out in the middle of the sea with some drug-runner who none of us knew the first fucking thing about.

'You won't need it,' I said. 'But you take it anyhow.'

I zipped the bag closed then eyed her intently.

'You need to go,' I said.

She paused, then brushed her hand against my cheek. Her fingertips warm against my skin.

I held her look a moment, then knelt down in front of Martin. 'I'll see you again. I promise.'

He put his arms around me.

'You're your own man, Martin. Remember that,' I said. 'You're better than all of us.'

As he gazed at me, I held his face in my hands.

A second burst of flame erupted on the Boulevard as another fuel tank exploded.

'If we're going, let's go,' said Bodie.

I picked Martin up and placed him on the deck of the boat, his eyes fixed on me as Alice led him down into the cabin. The moment they were inside, Bodie slid the roof hatch shut. A second later he revved the engine, the sleek nose arcing around in the water like a clock hand. With a plume of spray the boat surged away from the jetty and into the darkness. I kept my eyes on it until it was nothing more than a scratch in the moonlight. It finally disappeared from sight. I crouched down and tried to gather myself – it felt like my heart was firing on twelve faulty cylinders. As I caught my breath, Willard ran across the beach toward me.

He slowed and glanced back at the Boulevard. 'They haven't called in yet, I don't know what's happened.'

I got back to my feet and stared at the flames. 'We go up there.'

He eyed me a moment, then nodded.

'I need another weapon,' I said.

As I checked my pockets, I felt Alice's phone against my fingertips. She'd left it behind, but maybe that wasn't so bad if she was looking to make a clean disappearance. I took it from my pocket, ready to toss it into the sea, then paused a second. A message glowing on the home screen. It was from Janet McRae, the woman I'd questioned about who might have rented the cabin after the Samantha Lederer's death.

I read the message, my heartbeat fading to nothing as I tried to grasp the meaning of it.

My husband recalled another detail about the man who offered $10,000 to rent the cabin. He drove a blue vintage Mustang. I hope this is of some use to you. Janet McRae.

I just gazed at the message, a crushing weight bearing down on me. It felt like the jetty was collapsing beneath me.

I couldn't get my head around it. Willard?

He stared at me. 'What is it?' he said.

My blood like ice.

'Michael?' he said.

I slowly raised my head and gazed at him. I couldn't believe it.

His mood shifted as he eyed me uneasily. 'Michael?'

I kept my eyes on him.

He stepped toward me. 'Give me the phone.'

My voice flat, like it was prerecorded. 'It's nothing.'

But he was moving to a different tune now. His tone turned icy. 'Michael? Give me the phone.'

As I went to delete the message, he aimed his pistol at me. He stepped forward, held the barrel to my face, then reached for the phone. As he grabbed it from me, I pushed the pistol away from my face.

'You motherfucker,' I said.

He took aim at me again, my blood pounding as I got ready to dive into the sand just behind me.

'Don't move,' he said.

He kept the pistol aimed at me as he read the message, then closed his eyes.

'You killed all those people,' I said.

He shook his head.

'You killed them,' I said.

He sighed. 'I didn't know the family would be there, Michael.'

'You didn't know? And the others? Will Jerome?'

He laughed wearily to himself. 'I didn't even know who Jerome was. Lucky break for me Lenny Tripps was an enemy of his. I just needed to shut Lenny up and all this would have been over.'

I eyed the pistol in his hand. I was still too close. I needed to keep him talking.

'And Samantha Lederer? I said.

He shrugged. 'The heart is weak.'

'You were involved with her?'

He shook his head again.

'My father was,' he said. 'He used to go skiing in Gainsboro... got involved with her. She threatened to tell my mother. I was visiting him at the cabin the day she turned up. I wasn't about to let that peasant ruin him.'

'You killed her?'

'It got a little out of hand, admittedly. But you know how difficult these situations can get.' He took a deep breath. 'Now I have even more of this mess to clean up.'

I glanced back at the beach beside the jetty. As Willard stared philosophically at his gun, I stepped back onto the sand.

'What about the phone records? I said. 'That guy at the hotel we found?'

'You wouldn't tell me where Lenny was! I needed you to move against him... for you to do your job.'

'You've been killing people left, right, and center over this, haven't you?'

I stared at his pistol. He was losing his patience, but

I needed him to fire when I was ready.

'The ironic thing is, Michael… you'd actually have made a great agent. It's almost a shame to kill you.'

'Tell me, is your dad a fucking psychopath too?'

The venom bleeding out of him now. 'You don't know anything about my father.'

I eyed his hands. Anger makes us predictable, even a cold fish like Willard.

'I know he fucks young girls behind your mom's back,' I said.

'You're just making this easier for me to do, you know that?'

'I feel sorry for your mom. An unfaithful husband, a killer for a son. Who was her dad, the one idiot on the Hindenburg playing with matches?'

As he raised the gun, I dived backwards. The barrel sparking – the bullet zipping past me as I thudded onto the sand. I stared up at him as he calmly stepped toward to me, his shadow looming over me. As he took aim a final time, I uncurled the fingers of my right hand – the clip of his pistol lying in my palm. The single shot in the barrel, gone.

I grabbed a handful of sand and threw it into his face, his body toppling to the beach as I leaped onto him. He reached for a second gun in his ankle holster. I took hold of his arm. He grabbed at my head with his free hand and started jamming his thumb into my eye. As I strained to free myself, I grabbed at the gun in his hand. It fired.

I went still, my heart shuddering as I gazed down at him. The pressure in his clawed hand ebbed away – a thick stain spreading across his chest as his arm fell limp onto the sand.

I caught my breath, then got to my feet, his pistol hanging weakly from my fingers. As I bathed for a moment in the cool night air, I heard footsteps coming from the trees by the driveway. It took a firm hold of the gun and gazed into the shadows. Two figures emerged into the moonlight, one of them wounded being hauled along by the other. Klinger and Russo. They stopped dead as they caught sight of me down on the beach. Whoever they thought I was, I was standing over Willard's body with a gun in my hand.

They eyed me cautiously.

'You're Violet?' said one of them.

I gazed at them. Silent. Willard's blood seeping into the sand around my feet.

And in that split second I saw it all. My future. The glow of the flames lighting the sky around me like some harrowing dawn. Even if I could prove that Willard was responsible for all this, Southwest wouldn't care. The Oregon bombing was a national story – an investigation into one of their own would risk dragging the whole agency into the spotlight. The powers in DC would never allow that. Better to just kill me and be done with it. Standing over Willard's body with a smoking gun in my hand would be all the evidence they were ever going to be interested in. However this played out, I was going to be labeled an agent killer.

I'd have to run. And I'd never be able to stop.

As they reached for their guns, I turned and sprinted

for the trees. Toward the road and that terrible, burning
dawn.

15

I sat motionless in my hotel room chair, the afternoon rain pounding against the windows. The gray, metallic light of London casting cold shadows across the room. I gazed at my phone and waited for the call.

Three days since I'd escaped the Key, and everything I could salvage from my life was lying on the bed in front of me. A fake passport and credit card. A phone. A couple of photos of my mom and dad. And a little under eighteen thousand dollars. That was it.

I took a deep breath. I might have made it this far but there was no telling how much further I'd get. The world had a habit of rapidly shrinking when you were on the run. Distant cities suddenly knew your name. Even the wilderness had eyes for you.

I took a sip of whiskey and stared out of the window. As the gray light grew heavier, a tiny black shadow arced over the river. A solitary bird braving the rain. I watched as it soared across the bridges. Across the monuments and the spires. The air under its wings as it banked and swooped, unfettered by the world beneath it or the clouds above it. As it disappeared over the city, I rested my head again the window and closed my eyes.

The phone tugged me back to life as it rang.

I eyed the number. Andrew Toth from the London *Times*.

I answered the call. 'Hello?'

'Michael, it's Andrew. How are you?'

'Waiting.'

'I'm sure. Um... OK. I have some more questions. I was wondering if we could meet.'

'We do it like this.'

'Are you sure? It would be easier.'

'Like this,' I said.

'...OK.'

The shuffle of paper as he rifled through his notes at the other end of the line.

'Alright, I can't find Southwest Intelligence anywhere,' he said. 'There's Southwest Analytics, CEO Arlen Connell, but...'

'That's it. Analytics is the parent company. Southwest Intelligence is a division... the only division.'

'They're listed as consultants in political and international trade strategy.'

'What do you think they're going to list themselves as!'

'I know. But you have to understand, these are very serious allegations you're making. At the moment I have nothing to go on but the word of a self-confessed criminal.'

I took a calming breath. 'I'm not a thief any more. I told you, these are the skills they wanted. They...'

'But it's more than theft, Michael.'

I felt confused a second. 'What do you mean?'

'Are you aware you're currently named on an FBI Most Wanted List? In Florida, Illinois, and New York, you're wanted for murder.'

My eyes widened. Fuck.

'No. No, listen to me,' I said. 'This is Southwest trying to track me down. I've not been... I mean, I just... I don't even like New York!'

'You're telling me you've not killed any one, is that correct?'

'Not... not in any kind of... um...'

'I'm legally-bound to report this conversation now, do you understand?'

'Douglas Willard! Southwest Intelligence VP... fucking Analytics, whatever. This is who you need to look into! The man responsible for the Oregon bombing!'

'Douglas Willard has been reported dead... murdered while trying to apprehend you.'

I tried to gather myself.

'You think I'm making this up?' I said.

'To be honest, I don't know. If you could give me some evidence that this Southwest Intelligence agency actually exists, that would be a start. But as it stands I've really got no option but to bring the authorities in on this. I'm sorry.'

Fuck. It was going to be the same story no matter who I went to. The only evidence I had on Willard was hearsay that a vintage Mustang had show up in Gainsboro. As for Southwest, I couldn't even prove they existed. All my contact numbers were dead. The agency website no longer responded – just a blank page informing me that 'this URL doesn't exist'. They'd seemingly evaporated into the ether. Standard practice when one of their own turned against them, I guess.

Andrew's voice from the phone. 'Michael?'

This was a dead end for me. I hung up. I tossed the phone, then quickly scooped up my belongings from the bed and stuffed them into my jacket. I needed to get out of here – it was a good bet that Andrew had contacted the police already. As I crammed the last handfuls of cash into my pockets, I stared out at the skyline, then slowed a second. The stone landmarks of London in the distance. Maybe there was a way to corroborate my story. MI6's headquarters were just down the river. Southwest had ties to them, I think. Nothing too involved, but I'd definitely heard them mentioned at a couple of briefings. If there was any proof that Southwest existed, it might be there. It had to be. I'd have nothing otherwise. No credibility. No story. No option but to keep running.

Big Tim's Phone Repair shop sat just south of the river near Waterloo Station, the cramped shop's fluorescent lights glowing in the rain like mist. As I darted inside, a face appeared from behind a stack of old Samsungs – a weird-looking guy in his forties with the worst comb-ever I've ever seen. It looked like he grew his eyebrows and brushed them back.

'Can I help you?' he said.

I eyed the chaotic mess of phones under the glass counter. 'You got any used iPhone Xs?'

'What size?'

'Five point eight.'

It was the most common phone I'd seen used, certainly when it came to high-ranking executives and professionals.

'Any particular color?' he said.

'I need them all.'

'Right,' he said, a smile widening across his face.

He produced three bubble-wrapped iPhone Xs, peeled away the plastic, then laid them out on the counter.

'Silver, gray, and gold,' he said.

'How much?'

'Six hundred a piece. But they're unlocked, fully refurbished…'

'You got any that don't work?'

'Sorry?'

'I don't need them to work. The shittier they are, the better.'

'Er…'

He glanced at a pile of phones, SIM cards, and soldering irons on the worktop at the far end of the shop. 'I think I might have a silver and a gray. No gold though.'

'That's fine, I'll take them.'

'You sure? They really don't work at all.'

'Just give them to me.'

He reached back, then handed me the two phones. One gray, one silver. Both dead – one with a huge crack across its screen.

'How much?' I said.

He shrugged. 'Three hundred for both?'

I slapped the cash on the table, dropped the phone with the unbroken screen on the floor, then stamped on it until it cracked too. As I picked it back up, I glanced at the other broken phones on the worktop. A black Samsung S9 lying on the pile. It was a popular phone too – better to hedge my bets.

'Give me that Samsung as well,' I said.

I paid him another fifty, grabbed the phones, then headed out of the shop. I pulled the hood of my snorkel jacket way over my face and searched for a cab.

The MI6 building was a short ride away. A squat palace of stone and dark glass, it sat by the river like a cubist Buddha. Elegant in its own way, except for the ground floor which was surrounded by a steel wall. Armed police guarding the entrances to the building.

I stood in the shelter of a bus stop across the street from the main entrance, and waited. Nearly 12:30 – lunchtime for the British Secret Service. Standing at a bus stop with a plastic grocery bag full of shit phones, I doubted I'd have been any match for James Bond, but to each his own. As the rain eased up, the agency's staff began to emerge in fits and starts from the building. I eyed them carefully, a good proportion of them texting, talking, or checking their email as they walked. I caught sight of a couple of iPhones, but their owners were too young. In their late twenties. I needed someone older, higher up the ranks with greater security clearance.

As a group of young suits emerged from the entrance, I caught sight of a man and woman just behind them. The man was young, in his early thirties – but the woman was in her fifties. As the two of them chatted, the woman produced a phone and dialed a number. A silver iPhone X. My eyes widened as I gazed at it. I grabbed the matching phone from my bag, dumped the rest in a trash can, then crossed the road and followed after her.

I kept my eyes on her as I tailed her down the street. Getting Alice's phone had been easy, it was just her phone. But this was MI6. If they lose phones or laptops it's a security issue. They'd be a lot more vigilant as a result, plus I needed the phone unlocked – no risk that they'd set an instant lock screen. The question being, how do you take someone's phone while they're using it without them realizing it's gone?

I ran past the woman. 'Taxi!' I said.

As I raised my arm to wave down the cab, I knocked the phone from her hand – sliding it up my sleeve as I dropped its broken counterpart onto the ground from my other hand.

The woman stared down at the broken iPhone lying on the pavement. 'Oh, for God's sake!'

I turned to her. 'Shit, I'm sorry.'

'Why don't you look where you're going!'

She bent down and picked up the phone.

I eyed her sheepishly. 'Is it OK?'

She tapped at the broken screen but the phone remained as dead as it had been before. 'Oh, fucking hell.'

'I'm so sorry,' I said. 'Here, let me give you some money.'

She shot me a look, then sighed irritably. 'Just... just...'

She turned to the young guy beside her. 'Get Wallace to bring a new phone. Give me yours.'

As the guy handed her his phone, she stared at me. 'Watch where you're going! Idiot!'

I nodded – then jumped into the cab.

The driver glanced at me in rearview mirror. 'Where to?'

'Just drive,' I said.

As he pulled away from the river, I slipped the phone from my sleeve, and immediately pulled open the woman's email accounts. MI6 would have its own dedicated server – password-protected – but chances are her phone would be logged in already. I opened an account marked SIS – Secret Intelligence Service. I typed 'Southwest Intelligence' into the search bar then hit the button. The tiny wheel spun on the screen as the phone scanned the account. As the wheel twisted on and on I kept my eyes glued to the screen, praying that something would show.

The wheel disappeared, a message appearing in its place: 'No results found.'

I closed my eyes. Fuck.

I took a deep breath, then stared back at the phone. The woman had another three email accounts, but I seriously doubted she'd be communicating anything relevant via Gmail. I searched the accounts anyhow.

Nothing.

I had no proof at all.

As I gazed desolately out of the cab window, the driver glanced at me.

'You know where you're going yet?' he said.

I shook my head then stared back at the phone. I eyed it curiously for a second – maybe I was searching for the wrong thing. I reopened the SIS account and typed 'Southwest Analytics' into the search bar.

I gazed intently at the screen as the wheel started to spin again.

'Come on, come on,' I whispered.

The wheel continued to turn, its tiny gray spokes lazily rotating.

A message then appeared. 'One result found.'

My heart jumped a gear as I tapped it open. A single email from Southwest Analytics to a number of recipients at MI6 – dated yesterday.

But this was no proof that Southwest Intelligence existed. Instead, alarm bells rang through me as I read it.

Please be informed that one of our operatives will be arriving in London tomorrow afternoon. Traveling under the name H. L. Reed, they'll be arriving at Heathrow at 15:40. If you could offer them any assistance they might require, I'd be most grateful. Yours sincerely, Arlen Connell.

Jesus. They'd tracked me to London already.

I had to get out now. There was nothing left for me to do but run. I stared at the name: H. L. Reed. Not that that told me much. The hitmen at Southwest had more identities than they had surgical gloves. But he was arriving at 15:40. I needed to see his face. If I was going to have any chance of surviving, I needed to know who to watch out for in the crowds and shadows.

I glanced at the driver. 'Take me to Heathrow Airport.'

The only US flight arriving at 15:40 was from Chicago. At 16:20 I stood alone outside the giant terminal window, my eyes fixed on Arrivals. Torrential rain hammering onto the sidewalk around me. Mist rising from the paving stones and rooftops. I watched as families and couples emerged from the warmly-lit doors of the arrivals gate, my face a shadow under the soaking hood of my jacket.

As a steady stream of suits and tourists rolled through the doors, I searched for anyone traveling alone. I tried to picture the file photos of Southwest hitmen that I'd seen, but what few memories I had of their appearance were hazy and hard to pin down. I hoped that seeing them in the flesh would trigger some memory, or that I'd somehow manage to identify them just by their demeanor.

A businessman in his late thirties rolled out from the gate. Cropped black hair. Black suit. As he calmly glanced around the terminal I studied his features and waited for any distant sense of recognition to echo through me. A young woman with two small children then scurried through the crowds, and threw their arms around him. I let him be and returned my attention to the gate. Another figure traveling alone. An elegantly dressed woman – an Audrey Hepburn type, all pearl earrings, black heels, and dark glasses. As she wheeled her suitcase through the gate, a man in his forties appeared behind her. Casually dressed. Athletic build. He scanned the arrivals lounge, then nodded toward a waiting taxi driver who was holding up a board with his name written on it: Philip Rose. The name may not have matched, but there was something about the guy's appearance I didn't like. A cold detachment in his expression. I kept my eyes on him as he followed the driver toward the main exit. As he crossed the terminal, he passed by the Audrey Hepburn woman standing in the middle of the crowds. The woman dialed a number on her phone, then took off her sunglasses.

My heart stopped.

I couldn't breathe.

Ella.

She looked almost unrecognizable under all the glossy hair and make-up. But it was her. That ghostly beauty. Those dark, piercing eyes.

They'd sent her to kill me? I had no doubt that she had it in her to do it. But I couldn't think what to do.

As I gazed at her, she spoke into her phone – nodding casually as she glanced at the crowds drifting around her. She looked toward the windows, her gaze sweeping passed me as she searched for someone – a driver maybe. She paused a second. As she continued speaking into her phone, she slowly turned and stared back at the window – at my soaked, shadowy form beyond the glass. As she eyed me curiously, I took a step away from the glass. She lowered her phone, focused on me a second, then ran for the exit. A sense of movement around me now. Speeding figures emerging from the parking garage opposite the terminal. Two guys leaping over the concrete barriers, reaching into their jackets as they headed for me. I turned and darted through the crowds, sliding across car hoods as I dashed for the roads and the hazy, rain-soaked fields in the distance.

The thunder raging above me.

I ran.

Acknowledgements

Many thanks to Greg, Katrin, Hazel and all at Accent Press.

To Dave Savage for his weirdness and inspiration. And to Josh Peck for his insight and attention to detail. Much appreciated.

About The Author

Born in London, Alex pursued a writing career that took him to Los Angeles where he created shows for Disney, Universal and NBC.

After five years in LA, and the constant request for him to come up with a vampire show that was 'kind of like The Office', Alex decided to write something purely for his own pleasure.

The result is the Michael Violet Thrillers. He is currently writing the third novel in the series.

Proudly published by Accent Press

www.accentpress.co.uk